THE RIP'S MARK

R. S. K. ARCHER

CRANTHORPE MILLNER PUBLISHERS

First published by Cranthorpe Millner Publishers (2025)

ISBN 978-1-80378-327-7 (Paperback)

www.cranthorpemillner.com

Cranthorpe Millner Publishers

For my husband Alan,
who believed this was possible,
and for our two children,
who ensure we start every day early.

Hiding in a tree was certainly not on my to-do list today, yet here I am. The gaggle of teenage boys below angers me more than frightens me. I'm fairly certain I could take them, but not without seriously injuring a few. They aren't worth the bother.

I toy with one of my training knives instead, tossing it up and catching it by the blunted blade, whilst craning my neck to look for my dropped tablet – great day to forget my phone. Cassie and I are supposed to be training right now, and I need to message her to say I'll be a little late. These boys better hurry up and move on.

Turning my attention to my arm holster, I realise the third buckle is loose again. *Dammit.* I try and tie it closed to keep it from flapping, but it's a lost cause. I'll need to replace it as soon as I can afford to.

Restlessness fills my veins; adrenaline still pumping through me after being chased into the forest. I glare down at the unaware faces below; they're now resorting to shaking random trees and laughing incessantly. Maybe they're high on something? They wouldn't be nearly so confident if they were separated.

I rest my head back against my tree, knowing I'm too high up for them to find me. I'll just have to wait them out. I doze slightly and it's not long before all I can hear are the delicate sounds of birds returning to their nests as the sun begins to set. I glance at my watch and see I'm half an hour late to meet Cassie. She'll be worried. She always worries.

Jumping down from the tree, I land on silent feet, searching the surrounding area for my tablet. Dusting it off, I send a brief message to Cassie, apologising and telling her I'm on my way. I don't explain why – she'll make too big a deal over it.

I step out from the cluster of trees and onto the country track heading into my village, and I almost walk straight into one of the boys. We both jump back and stare in surprise at each other. It's Edward. The colour drains from his face and fear fills his eyes. I thought I saw his head amongst the group chasing me, but this confirms it.

He takes a step back and glances behind him, perhaps hoping some of the others are nearby. I open my mouth to say something; maybe this is my chance to finally get him to see how stupid and ignorant those idiots he hangs out with are. But before I can utter a word, he sprints past me, only looking back once to see if I'm following. I can't believe he genuinely thinks I'd hurt him! We were friends when we were little kids, but that all changed once we started secondary school and he made friends with those OWL – other world – haters. I shake my arms to get rid of the last burst of adrenaline and make a beeline for home to meet Cassie.

Sticking to the high street so I'm in plain view of everyone – I really don't want a repeat of what just happened – I find Cassie sitting on my fence chatting to her girlfriend. Sarah is a sweet girl with long, dark curly hair, wide blue eyes and dark skin, whilst Cassie is her polar opposite, both in personality and looks. Her cute, curly strawberry blonde hair is at odds with her fiery temper, and her dark eyes always look like she's plotting something. Their height is the only thing they have in common, both barely reaching my shoulders. I really do like Sarah and am over-the-moon happy that Cassie has found someone she loves – and who helps keep her calm. However, it's very clear Sarah is uncomfortable around me. She's never said anything about it, at least not to me, but she never tries to hang out with us, and I can see that bothers Cassie.

"Indie! Finally, what on earth took you so long? Is everything okay?" Cassie asks.

"Everything's fine, just got held up."

"Do I want to know why you have leaves stuck in your hair, or are we going to pretend like you haven't been napping in a tree?"

"I'm good with pretending," I reply, trying my best to give her a reassuring smile but knowing I've failed.

Cassie raises an eyebrow at me, but she knows me too well to push. There isn't much she can do, and stirring the pot has definitely not worked out for us in the past.

Right on cue, Sarah quickly makes her excuses and leaves us to commence our training. I'm secretly glad she's heading home, as this is our last night of freedom before I start at the Luenn Academy and Cassie starts at college, and I would like her all to myself.

I slap Cassie playfully on the thigh. "Come on then, let's do one final training session before I get too hungry."

Cassie snorts in response, hopping over the fence towards my makeshift training ground in the back garden.

Thwack!

Damn! Missed it.

"You're not using your Tk," Cassie's singsong voice calls out from behind me, with a trace of indifference.

"Not when it hurts like a…"

"I've heard of people who can move bridges without even a twinge."

Growling in response, I hurl my last knife at the distant target. I give it the slightest nudge, using my very limited Telekinesis, Tk, so it lands bang centre of the target, but, boy, does it hurt. I grind my teeth whilst my brain feels like it's trying to force its way out of my skull. However, my throwing knife did make a very satisfying *thunk* as it landed in the tree twenty metres away. I give my temples a gentle rub with the tips of my fingers and glance at Cassie.

"Nice," she says, sitting on my deck chair, drinking my lemonade, and reading her book.

"You didn't even see it. If you would take your nose out of that book for half a second, you'd notice that shot was more than just nice."

Cassie tosses her hair out of her face to glance at the tree. "Very nice," she says.

I roll my eyes and trudge off to collect my three knives, two of which, thankfully, made it into the tree. Yanking them out, I place them back into my arm holster.

I took a weapons training course at school last year, and felt drawn to the knives as soon as I saw them, likely because they were my mother's weapon of choice, it's her old holster I'm wearing. As soon as I started throwing them, I felt a wave of something that was almost like an electric charge. A sensation of completion and connection to the knives themselves that ran through my body. It's hard to explain as I'd never experienced it before but, in essence, it felt right.

I turn to head back up to the house, and notice Cassie still has her nose firmly clamped between the pages of her romance book – she's a sucker for same-sex romance fiction. My lips quirk up to the side as an idea pops into my head.

I slowly slink back into the knot of trees at the bottom of the garden and edge around to the left. Unlike me, Cassie is fully Earthborn and so doesn't hear or notice my approach – one of the side effects of my rather unique DNA is that I can move very fast. I manage to race around to the back of her chair, grabbing her book as I jump over her side table, and land gracefully onto the deckchair opposite. All before she even realises what's happening. I smile and reach across to the little table beside her to grab her sandwich. Taking a large bite, and ignoring her gasp of protest, I turn her book to the last page and start reading aloud. Cassie shrieks, jumps up and clamps her hands over her ears. Laughing, I stop reading and quickly eat the rest of her chicken salad sandwich, whilst giving her a completely innocent look.

"Indigo!" Cassie yells as she grabs her drink and tries to throw it over me.

I manage to dodge the drink but, sadly, my chair does not. I glare up at her, and Cassie grins back. "Well," I say, "since you've finished your sandwich and drink, do you want to help me train now?"

Cassie has been my training partner since I knew I wanted to be a guardian, so pretty much forever. She's my best and, really, only friend. The other kids growing up were all, at best, wary of me and at worst, downright hostile. Cassie's family were close to my father's, and so Cassie and I grew up more as sisters than friends.

My mother and Cassie's were very close, before my mother

was killed when I was two. Cassie's mum still likes telling me little stories about her. I think the topic of my mother is too painful for my father to talk about, so I rarely bring it up with him. Anytime I do find out anything new about my mum, I immediately write it down. I know so little; any and every detail is precious.

My mother, Elna, was put up for adoption at a very young age on Evig, her home world, and her adopted parents died before she finished her guardian training. Consequently, there is no one there I know of who could tell me more about who she was and where I come from. Thinking about my mum is like falling down a dark spiral staircase lined with photos of her face. I feel it drawing me down to that warm yet almost empty place in my mind.

Grief is a weird thing. It's not so much missing the person but missing the person they could have become and the person you could have been with them. I want her to be proud of me, but I am also glad she doesn't know I'm about to embark on the very same career that got her killed. It certainly doesn't sit well with my father.

Shrugging off those thoughts and the echoes of arguments with my dad, I look up to see Cassie watching me, her knowing, dark eyes soft and sad before she seems to mentally shake herself.

She slaps my boot-clad foot and says, "Come on then, Indie. Now you've finished your first dinner, you might actually move slow enough for me to hit you."

She looks way too happy about that idea. I jump out of my chair, trot down to the bottom of the garden and turn to face Cassie, who stays where she is, slightly elevated by the decking. She needs the added height, given she's a little vertically challenged, in complete contrast to me. I catch my reflection in the patio doors. I'm dressed head to toe in black: black stretch trousers tucked into my calf-high soft black leather boots, and a black, skin-tight sleeveless top. My long dark hair is tied high on my head. My wardrobe mostly consists of black clothes that allow for movement. I'm standing with my feet slightly apart, balancing on the balls of my toes, with my fists placed about chin height. I look ready, certainly ready for this session, but for the Luenn Academy? I'm not entirely sure.

The first knife I easily see coming and have no trouble dodging. The second and third are thrown simultaneously and require a little more attention. I dodge into the path of the one on my right, to avoid the one on my left, and use my Tk to cause the one heading towards my face to alter its course by about five degrees. Handy, but it would be so much more useful if I could alter it, say, by 180 degrees. The pain caused by that tiny shift settles into the back of my skull and gradually increases as I use my Tk more and more. I've tried pushing hard against the pain in my head before, but it doesn't seem to make any difference to the strength of my Tk, only to the pain. I've been told my tutor specialises in Tk training at the Academy, but that only makes me anxious, as most people I've met haven't come across someone who demonstrates Tk at any cost to themselves.

The knives Cassie flings my way are slightly blunted, but not enough for me to block without injury. I could wear my protective gear, but it's early afternoon in September and far too warm for that. So, I'm left to dodge and nudge with my mind. It's exhausting. With sweat beginning to trickle down my back, I call time fifteen minutes in. I'm tired from the training I did earlier, and from the rather epic migraine that's trying to worm its way in behind my right eye – why always my right?

"Not bad. I know I'm not fast, but you were merely a blur to me. Were you even using your Tk?"

"I tried not to overuse it, but, yes, the aftereffects are definitely making themselves known."

"How long do you think it'll take to clear?" Cassie asks whilst tidying up the mess she and I made on the decking.

"Probably ten minutes or so. It doesn't feel as bad as that one from yesterday." The length of time spent using my Tk really affects how long my migraines last. There's no easing off, one minute I need to lie down in the dark and the next it's gone. Thinking of which, I lie down on the grass, close my eyes and wait for this one to pass. I sling my right arm over my eyes to shade them from the setting sun and listen to Cassie as she moves about collecting the fallen knives. She comes to lie down next to me.

"I can't help but think this is goodbye," she says.

"I'll still have some evenings free, I imagine, but, yeah, it'll be weird not seeing you every day. Although," I mutter, "not being associated with a freak at your college will likely do something for your social standing."

"You know I don't like you calling yourself that, and besides, I'm pretty sure there will be some other OWLs there too for me to associate with. Got to keep fighting the good fight."

Even though I'm only half other-world, that small taint in my DNA has always been enough for me to be socially ostracised. Now I'm going to study in a place where there'll be people from all over our world who are like me, or at least willing to work alongside all types of OWLs.

"I'm really happy for you, Indigo. I know how much this means to you and you've certainly worked hard for it. However, I am selfishly glad we live so close to the Academy that you can still live at home."

"Me too," I reply, turning my head towards her and smiling slightly. The thought of leaving home feels like a leap into the unknown that I don't think I'm ready for. I know I'll have to do some training up in Scotland, so that will give me some experience, and then maybe next year I'll live on campus. Most students have to live on campus as they rarely live this close to Cambridge. In fact, many come from overseas and a few are even other-world.

Cassie sits up with a groan. "I actually had better go. My mum wants me home for dinner tonight, so I'll have to love you and leave you."

Reaching down, she pats me lightly on the arm covering my face.

"You'll do great tomorrow, Indie. I just know it."

Grinning at her, I wave goodbye and promise to call her tomorrow night to tell all.

As I lie on the grass, the early evening sun warms my legs and my migraine rapidly fades. Feeling much better now I'm headache-free, I go inside to investigate what my dad's planning for dinner – yes, this will technically be my second. He's a pretty good cook, so I tend to leave that to him. My need to continuously eat has led me to become an expert sandwich maker, cheese toasties being my favourite, but anything that takes more than fifteen minutes is more than I have the patience for.

Walking up to the back door, I hear the radio blaring before I'm enticed by the smell of his infamous spaghetti bolognese. Definitely my favourite meal of all time. I enter the kitchen and see my dad with his back to me as he stirs the pots on the hob. I grab a teaspoon from the drawer on his left, making him jump slightly there was no way he could have heard me entering the kitchen with the music playing so loudly. I dip the spoon into the sauce, blow lightly on it and take a taste. Delicious. I'd ask him what his secret is but, given I have no intention of ever making it, I don't bother.

"You're right on time, I'm about to dish up. I take it Cassie's not staying?"

"Excellent, and no, Cassie just left. She's having dinner with her mum tonight."

I start laying the table, pouring the water into our weighty tumblers and hunting for the ever-elusive pepper grinder. As we sit down to eat, I can feel my father's gaze on me. I know people like to talk and eat at the same time, but I really like to focus on getting the food inside me first. Then I can pay attention to the conversation, and not to my empty stomach. I have a sense I won't be allowed to do that today.

Glancing up, I ask, "What is it?"

"Nothing. I think I'm only now realising this is actually going to happen, and I'm not going to be able to change your mind."

"You're only figuring this out now?" I reply, incredulous, as I watch him slowly twist the spaghetti around his fork.

"Well… yes. I guess I felt that when push came to shove, you'd realise what you were getting yourself into and stay well clear. But evidently, that isn't going to happen, either because you're unwilling to see the danger, or worse, you see it and think your life is worth risking."

I stop eating and stare at him. "I really don't know what to say. This is what I want to do, what I've always wanted to do. I thought we'd already talked this through."

"We have, but I was still hopeful you'd change your mind. Apparently, that isn't an option for you and forbidding you to continue would only lead you to follow a similar and likely less safe path when you're older, so here we are."

He looks directly into my eyes, almost willing me to disagree and say that if he forbade it, I'd find some safe office job instead. But I don't. The silence stretches well beyond comfort: we're at a standoff. If I show even the slightest hesitation, he will use that as a reason not to support me. At only seventeen, I need his consent to commence my training. I could wait a year, but then I'd be behind my peers and without financial support. Both of which would jeopardise my training and my ability to compete for a top position. I remain as calm as possible and look right back at him.

Eventually, he grimaces ever so slightly, sighs, and goes back to his meal.

Sighing silently myself, in relief, I go back to devouring my dinner. I hate that this has put such a strain on our relationship, but I know what I'm doing is right for me and that I have potential, and ultimately a duty to be of great help to our world.

Later that night, when we've finished binge-watching TV together, I head up to my room to sleep. After brushing my teeth in the bathroom, I glance at my reflection in the mirror. I look tired, which is somewhat unsurprising given the hour and the length of time I spent training today. The bright lights of the bathroom give my already pale skin an eerie, translucent quality, and makes my dark blue eyes look even closer to the colour indigo, which I'm named after. I stick my tongue out at my reflection and head into my bedroom.

My room is quite small, only fitting a single bed, and the lack of space isn't helped by the numerous posters I have on my walls. Every wall has at least half a dozen posters of different landscapes from different worlds. Since the creation of the Rip back in the '70s, by a rather clueless chemistry student up in Scotland, the world has been fascinated by what we've found on the other side – and by what has come through. Earth was lucky that Evig's people were the first to realise we had created a Rip. They then came through to advise us and set up a structure to protect us from invaders, whilst allowing us to control where the Rip took us.

Evig, we believe, was the first Earth-like planet to discover a Rip on its surface and use it to find other worlds living in parallel universes. Some of these 'rips,' so called as they literally look like a rip through space, were created by striking asteroids or by a rather catastrophic accident. No one knows how to create one, as no one has survived the process.

The ambassadors from Evig helped set up the Luenn Academy, which trains guardians to, essentially, guard and control our Rip. This is what I want to do. It's a dangerous job, and people from other Earth-like planets can have a wide variety of physical advantages, which is why people like me are often recruited for these roles.

My mother died whilst protecting our world, so I fully understand the risks. But who knows who might try to come and take advantage of us and our resources, or what they might bring with them? Training as a guardian is not only what I want to do, it's what I feel I must do.

Chapter 2

My jeans are ripped. I caught them whilst riding my bike to the Academy. It's my first day and I'm already having a wardrobe malfunction. Hopefully, people will think the two slashes across my left calf are a deliberate fashion choice.

The Luenn Academy is right in the centre of town, a half-hour cycle from my village. It's perhaps an odd location, given the Rip is over three hundred miles north, in Scotland, but with the wide-open countryside surrounding the city, it's the perfect spot for training. The real reason it's located here is rumoured to be because the man who set it up back in the late '70s lived in the area and didn't wish to move his family. He also happened to purchase, with the help of the newly set up council, the most beautiful and unusual building. It was originally used as a hospital but, after it moved to the south side of the city, the building needed a new purpose.

Located near the centre of Cambridge, on Trumpington Street, it really stands out from the rest of the period buildings. Set back from the road, the tree-lined path leads to an impressive, pale-bricked four-storey building, three times as wide as it is tall, and lined with arched columns and windows. The accents of red and blue brick hint at the array of colours inside. I've always loved this building. Admittedly, that's because it's where I've always dreamed of attending. Cycling up the path, I feel excited but with a sense of trepidation. I really don't want to mess this up.

I lock my bike to the side of the building and finally get to take my first steps through the double doors. The wall of sound from all the other students milling around the floors above hits me with remarkable force, shortly followed by the intense colour scheme and architecture. Everywhere I look, there are stripes of red, blue and yellow against a backdrop of white tiles and pale wooden floors. There appears to be a pattern to the different colours: most of the stripes are horizontal, so maybe they're supposed to lead you somewhere? Circles also dominate the space, from the windows to the doors, in varying sizes. The effect is unusual but welcoming.

As I look around, I quickly realise there is a queue forming in front of a remarkably calm, and very beautiful, young guy. Not wanting to be the last to check in, I swiftly join it. I look down and spot a bright pink piece of paper taped to the floor, informing me this is the first years' registration queue. Thank goodness I don't need to sidle out of it and look like an idiot.

I reach the desk, give the man a small smile and tell him my name. Smiling in return, he starts scanning his list. The sticky label on his shirt tells me his name is Jed, and he looks fairly Earthborn, with tanned skin, bright blond hair and blue eyes. The American accent is also a giveaway, although he could have been brought up there.

"Aha, Indigo Walker, there you are. Here's your pack. It's got your forms, maps, course details, etcetera inside, a very handy pen and an impractically small, monogrammed notepad. Here's your Academy ID card, which you really don't want to lose or then you won't be able to enter any of the rooms in this building or the training grounds."

I take the ID card from him and smile in thanks.

Leaning back, he says, "Now you need to head along to Lecture Theatre A for your introduction talk. Welcome to Luenn Academy, Indigo."

"Thanks, Jed," I reply.

He gives me another smile, only this one seems more genuine as it reaches his eyes, causing his smooth skin to crinkle slightly. I move to the side to let the person behind me come forward. Whilst I negotiate my way around the desk in search of Lecture Theatre A, I catch him giving me the once-over out of the corner of my eye. Pretending I don't notice, I move forward and spot a group of lost souls heading towards a large, again, pink, sign with a giant capital 'A'. As good-looking as Jed is, I really don't wish to get involved with anyone, however casually. This year is all about hard work.

I follow the steady flow of first year students, looking at their faces to try and determine where they're from and what their special skills are. Sometimes you can tell because they'll have distinctive traits, with a unique colouring, size or body shape. My pale skin and dark hair, although common on many different worlds, is particularly prevalent on Evig. Many of the people there have eyes and skin that are overly sensitive to light, so they spend a lot of time inside. Thankfully, I didn't inherit the sensitive eyes, but my very pale skin is a bit of a giveaway. Cassie calls it translucent, but I say it's corpse-like. Seriously, I practically glow in the dark and always need a generous lathering of sunscreen just to leave the house in summer. At least it makes buying makeup easy: just choose the palest shade and it'll be almost light enough.

So far, almost every world's dominant species has been a version of what we think of as human. However, I did hear there was one world where there was very little wildlife, and it appears they had, relatively recently, undergone an apocalyptic event. There is also a world ruled by an alien species from a nearby solar system, who completely dominate and refuse to let people from the other worlds through their Rip – they shoot and don't ask any questions.

I enter the semi-circular tiered lecture theatre and take a seat not too far from the emergency exit. I've been in situations that required a rapid exit, usually after some idiot discovers my heritage, so I've learned to scope out all possible exits when I enter a new space. Of all the places I've been, this is where I should be and feel safest, but old habits die hard.

Flipping through the pack of materials Jed gave me, I locate the documents detailing the courses for this year and have a quick scan through. The Luenn Academy is quite secretive about how they train their guardians. I've already had to sign a non-disclosure agreement stating that I'll never discuss anything that goes on inside the Academy with anyone from the outside. This is largely to prevent the public from becoming alarmed about the abilities some of the guardians possess, and how – and where – they demonstrate them. I'm allowed to talk about my fellow students in general terms, but not their skill sets, their names or what the training specifically involves. This was definitely a hard one for Cassie as she, like everyone else, is desperately curious about what goes on behind these doors. Thankfully, as I'm still a minor, my dad was able to sign one too, so I have at least one person outside of the Academy I can talk things through with. I'm excited that I'm finally going to find out exactly what I'll be learning and no longer have to hide who I am.

The first page that catches my eye is about weapons training. There are a huge variety of weapons we'll be working with.

According to the short description, it's because some of us will be travelling to other worlds to work alongside their guardians and need to be trained with their approved weapons.

One of the rules we have across all worlds is that we do not bring across new technology, including weapons, unless there has been a trade agreement made between the two worlds' councils. This means, as there are some worlds which are quite technologically primitive, we'll be working with knives and bows and arrows, alongside the more advanced weapons. The lessons involving the use of knives, unsurprisingly, grab my attention most.

I start to flick through the rest of the documentation when a very familiar face walks in and stands, facing us, at the front of the lecture theatre. Ivy Jenkins.

Ivy is my hero. Although fully Earthborn, she's worked her way up from the admissions department to becoming Head of the Luenn Academy and sitting on our world's council. Very impressive, considering she's only thirty-four years old. She's also the first woman to hold this position and has been a great public campaigner for OWL's rights. At six feet tall, she is powerfully built, with long, straight blonde hair and hazel eyes. Those eyes are currently surveying the students in front of her, who are all looking increasingly nervous.

When her eyes sweep to my side of the room, I feel their impact. She really does look like she takes no prisoners. Seeming both satisfied and slightly disappointed with the lack of reaction – were we supposed to clap? – she begins her speech.

"Welcome, Class of 2030. You are here because you have proven that not only are you the best in your generation, but that you have the determination and drive to make our world safe and open to others. It's not about your heritage, it's about what you, as an individual, can offer this organisation and this world.

"We have a wealth of experience here to get the best out of you. Some of our practices may seem a little tough, but that's what many of you will face when you leave here to start work.

"The Luenn Academy moulds you into your best self. So even if, after your two years here and your subsequent probationary year, you decide this isn't the right path, you will still have an abundance of experience and skills to help improve our world in some other capacity.

"Although my role on the council is very important, I still spend most of my time at the Academy, and my door is always open to those who need me. We also have a very capable team here who will do their best for you, so let me introduce you to Head of First Year Training, Connor Fischer."

This time, we all clap.

Mr Fischer stands up from the front row, shakes Ivy's hand and turns to face us. Wow. This is definitely someone I do not wish to cross. He looks like someone told him one of us is holding his pet dog hostage, and he's going to glare at us until someone confesses. He's striking, with high cheekbones and colouring that suggests a Native American heritage, and his short dark hair and all-black jeans and T-shirt give off a strong military vibe.

He's completely silent, and I realise with unease that he's staring at each of us in turn. Okay, this is seriously intense. What is it with the dominance games this morning? As I watch those he's looking at, I realise he's waiting for them to look away.

As he reaches my row, the two boys sitting beside me look away almost instantly. I'm tempted to do the same, to get this over with. But something inside me is stubborn. Okay, scratch that, I'm stubborn. Maybe if I glare back, instead of staring impassively, he'll move on quicker.

Nope. Oh, wow, this is hard.

His eyes are narrowing. I guess this is how he shows he's serious. I narrow mine too.

I sense those around me start to stare at me as well. I can't tell whether they're willing me to win this or whether they want me to stop so we can get this over with. I'm going to go with win, otherwise I might give up.

I've heard the expression, 'his eyes are piercing', but I've never fully understood it, until now. His eyes are actually hurting me, as if he's trying to shove needles into my own to get me to turn away. I really hope I don't have to spend too much time with this guy.

Okay, it has to have been at least a couple of minutes. I'm too far in to look away now. Should I say something? He's frowning, so probably not.

I decide not to mimic him and keep focused, trying not to look too stressed. Have I blinked? It feels like I have a thick layer of grit over my eyes.

At least another minute goes by before his lips quirk up to the side and he moves on to the person beside me. Did I win? Feels like I won. I can't tell whether the quirk of his lips was amusement or displeasure, but think it's best if I steer clear of him for the next few days and hope he forgets who I am. I imagine it's a bit too soon to draw too much attention towards myself.

For the rest of the staring contest, I focus my attention on Mr Fischer. Maybe he's actually doing something whilst he stares at us. Oh God, is he telepathic? What if he was reading my mind whilst we were so focused on one another? Did I think anything offensive? I have heard of telepaths before, but they are incredibly rare as they only originate from one world, and he doesn't have any of the recognisable physical traits that go with that world. But the staring has to mean something other than a show of his superiority. He looks way too sure of himself to be *only* human.

As I ponder his heritage, I realise the staring contest is over, and he has started to speak. He has a strong southern American accent, his lilting tones completely at odds with his stern exterior.

"You'll find out shortly who your training partner and your mentor are. You will be working very closely with these two people over the next two years, and they have been carefully chosen to both complement your strengths and challenge your weaknesses. In only extreme circumstances will you be moved from your group, so don't ask to be moved because of a personality clash. As head of first year training, I'll be paying close attention to your mentor's reports. It's a tough first year, so don't expect to be able to coast your way through. If we think you can do more, we'll make sure you do. If you continue not to work at your upper limit, you will be asked to leave.

"You are to look in your booklets and find out where your physical assessments are taking place and head there now. Once you have completed this, one of our helpers will tell you where to meet your partner and mentor. Good luck."

I think he wants us not to like him. It's working.

Looking in my pack, I spot the sheet detailing my physical assessment. It's on the first floor and there are changing rooms next door. There are four names written above mine, so at least I have some time to change and warm up. I have no idea whether 'physical assessment' means taking my blood pressure or measuring how fast I can run. The fact that there are changing rooms gives some of it away. I'm not entirely sure how they can test my speed indoors, as I really need a track to get up to speed.

It takes me a good ten minutes to locate the assessment and changing rooms, and another five to get ready. I've got my painkillers in my back pocket, in case they ask me to demonstrate my Tk. There's a little table and chairs set up outside the room on the galleried landing overlooking the reception area below. The four other students are already sitting there, waiting and reading through their materials. No one appears to be chatting, which is a bit strange, so I sit down with them on the only available chair and wait too.

Ten minutes later, Jed pops his head around the door and asks for Lucy. The tall blonde girl from our table stands up and heads towards him. Jed gives us all a tight smile, his eyes passing over each of us in turn, then heads back into the room. Did I imagine that he focused on me for a fraction of a second longer? Okay, I really don't want to think about this right now, so I need to distract myself.

I look over at the petite redheaded girl next to me and ask, "Do you know what kind of assessments they're doing in there?" I caught a glimpse of a treadmill and weights when Jed opened the door to let Lucy through but couldn't spot anything else.

"No idea," she replies. "My strongest skill is reaction time, and you don't need to do much physical exercise to demonstrate that." Turning in her seat to face me, she extends her hand. "I'm Miranda, by the way."

"Indigo. Nice to meet you." Shaking her hand, I notice she has a tattoo on each of her index fingers. I try and sneak a closer look to see what the tattoos are, but she quickly removes her hand and rests it on her lap, palm upwards.

"So, what are your 'special' skills?" she asks, using her fingers to illustrate the inverted commas. "You looked like you were trying to shoot laser beams out of your eyes when staring down Mr Fischer earlier."

Grimacing slightly, I reply, "Speed, strength, and a little Tk, although that doesn't really count because it's so small."

"Wow, speed and strength? You must not have to worry about much, physically I mean. Do you have Evig heritage? Forgive me for assuming, but with those skills and your skin tone it seems too obvious not to mention. Although the Tk is a little unusual."

"Yeah, my mum was Evigborn. Although, thankfully, I didn't inherit any sensitivity to light."

"Huh, that would be challenging here."

"So, since we're talking about it, what's your heritage and 'special' skills?" I ask, copying her use of air quotes.

"Well, now, that's the big question. My mum is fully Earthborn, but I never knew my father. My mum had a drunken one-night stand when she was celebrating Hogmanay in Edinburgh, so it must have been with an OWL. I can't say I'm not curious. My DNA doesn't point to one world in particular, so unless I happen upon him and realise who he is, I'll probably never know. But apart from the free visitor pass to that world, it doesn't really matter."

"Wow, I'm sorry you never got to know him."

"Yeah, but at least their carelessness got me here, so I feel pretty lucky too. The, uh, only other skill I have is mimicking, but I try to only use it if I have to."

"Miranda," Jed's voice calls from behind us.

I didn't even hear him open the door, I was so focused on what Miranda was saying. With a small smile, she heads into the room with Jed. Turning back to face the rest of the table, I see the two remaining guys studiously avoiding my gaze. Deciding to follow suit, I look back at my pack of information and try to figure out the layout of the building, so I don't get lost again. I really wish I got a chance to ask Miranda what a mimic was, I've never heard of one before. Does she mean in terms of someone's character, or perhaps she can even mimic someone else's talents? It would be seriously impressive, but surely too powerful for this programme; that sort of talent would certainly mean she'd be fast tracked to a different one.

The two guys ahead of me are called in pretty quickly, one after the other, and it's not long before Jed calls me in to be tested. Sitting here and waiting for my turn has definitely allowed my mind to wander and come up with some pretty elaborate and dangerous ways they could test me. But, really, I'm anxious they're going to try and push me to demonstrate my Tk. I don't want to have to deal with a migraine whilst meeting my partner and mentor. Grabbing my bags, I head towards Jed and the room behind him.

"You can leave your bags here," says Jed, gesturing to the chair on my left. "I just need you to read this over for me. Check your name and address are correct, and that you possess these skills and so are happy with us testing them."

Looking down at the list I spot my Tk, and it's noted as minor – thank goodness – along with my strength and speed. "I can get fairly crippling migraines when I use my Tk, so unless you have a dark room I can go lie down in afterwards, I don't want to push that one too far."

Jed glances up at the other two people in the room, who are now facing me. Clearly, they are in charge.

"That's okay, Indigo," says the older of the two women.

"We'll still need to check you possess it, but we won't push you too far today. We only really want to know what your limits are right now, so we can better prepare your training programme and log your improvement after each review."

"Ah, okay then," I reply, and take the pen out of Jed's outreached hand to sign the paper. I'm not entirely sure what she means by 'each review'. Maybe it's something they do each term? Hopefully not each week.

"Okay then, Indigo," says the younger of the two women. She has a vibrant stripe of red running through her hair, which is striking against her dark hair and skin. "Since your Tk might cause you some discomfort, we'll start with your speed test."

I snort faintly at the 'slight discomfort' remark but nod my head and look towards the mat she's gesturing towards. I glance back and realise Jed has already left the room, it's just me and the two examiners now. I walk towards the mat whilst looking around the room to see what I'm supposed to do, and spot the tennis ball-launching machine on the far-right wall. Reaching the mat, I turn and face it whilst glancing questioningly at the young woman. Am I about to play dodgeball?

A whirring sound starts from behind me, and I feel cool air race across my bare arms. Clearly, I'm expected to sweat with this workout. I usually love a cold environment, but I'm quite tense and the cool air is not really working for my already rigid muscles.

The older woman appears in my peripheral vision as she side-steps up to my left. Sweeping her long blonde hair off her shoulder, she pulls up her clipboard, tapping her pen against her teeth, whilst staring down at the paperwork in front of her. She glances across the room at the other examiner and asks her to turn the ball machine to level three. Then she looks back at me.

"It's quite a simple task. We need you to catch the balls and throw them into this basket over here." She points at a basket about six feet to the left of the ball machine. "Don't use your Tk, and try to conserve some energy in the beginning, as we will increase the speed. Good luck."

They both move to stand to the right of the machine, then the younger woman reaches down and flicks a switch. The machine starts off fairly slow, or at least slow for me. I move freely around the mat and start to get into the rhythm of watch, move, catch, throw, repeat. It's almost therapeutic. I tune out of my surroundings and focus on the job at hand.

The sound of the tell-tale clunk of the switch, which increases the speed, invades my bubble of calm. The balls are coming faster now, but I'm nowhere near my limit. It takes two more speed increases for me to really feel I'm tapping into my advanced speed. Now I truly start to enjoy myself. My lips pull into a slight smile as I revel in the feeling of my muscles stretching, my body twisting, and the satisfactory sound of the balls landing in the basket. As I go through the motions, a part of my mind – perhaps unhelpfully – is trying to puzzle out how the basket never gets full and there seems to be a never-ending supply of tennis balls. They must be connected in some way, but it is far from obvious. I continue to dance around the room at impressive speed, but I'm still not working at the top of my ability.

A minute later, they turn off the machine. The sudden stop causes me to stumble; I was expecting this to last longer, to get faster. The two women are looking at the older woman's tablet, muttering to each other. I catch a couple of snippets of their conversation.

"Maxed out."

"We don't have time for that."

"She's faster than him."

Glancing up at me, the younger woman's eyes narrow. "Can you move faster?" she asks.

"Yes," I reply. "I've only been able to max out when running on a track."

"Hmmm…" she replies. "We shall have to leave it there for now as we don't have time to take you out to the field. I'll let your mentor know he needs to test you."

Oh, yay for me.

"Since that took longer than expected," the older woman says, "and you're clearly warmed up, we're going to jump straight into weightlifting at quite a high level."

Walking over to the left-hand side of the room, we pass around a screen, likely placed there to stop any wayward tennis balls, and come to a row of heavily loaded barbells.

"Come over to these mats," she says. "You are to deadlift these one at a time. Stop when it gets uncomfortable. In this instance, we're not trying to max you out."

She indicates I'm to start halfway down the row. Working my way to the end of the row takes me little time and, annoyingly for them, little effort. When I finish the last lift of 300kg without so much as a puff of exertion, they call time. I really hope my mentor doesn't have to test me on this too.

The Tk assessment is next, and I'm far from looking forward to this. The younger woman explains that all I have to do is try to move the largest possible object on the table approximately one centimetre to the left. Looking at the table, I spy the usual suspects: a pencil, a book, a paperweight and small and large square-bottomed dumbbells.

Reaching out with my Tk, I test the objects to see if I can

shift them. I get as far as the paperweight before I really sense resistance, so I move it slightly to the left. That kind of looks like one centimetre.

As soon as I release it, I feel the pain. It's sharp and persistent. I won't need painkillers as it'll disperse in a few minutes, but I do ask if I can sit down and close my eyes whilst I wait it out. Sitting down on a chair by the door I came through, I close my eyes and wait for it to pass. I hear the women talking to each other, but I don't pay them any attention. It's too difficult to concentrate whilst the pain is holding my brain hostage.

As the pain lifts, a hand lands on my shoulder. Looking up, I see a concerned-looking Jed crouching down in front of me.

"Are you okay?"

"Yeah," I lie, "it's passed now. Are we finished?"

"You're free to go. Come, I'll take you to your mentor's room."

He grabs my stuff and hands it to me. Taking it from him, I sling my bag over my shoulder and give the women a small wave as I follow Jed out the door at the back of the room. Ah, this is why I never saw anyone leave the training room. As we walk down the corridor and up a couple of flights of stairs, Jed chats to me. Apparently, he's a second year and hoping to become a travelling guardian, rather than one focussing on intelligence or guarding the Rip. This is what I want to do as well, although I don't get to tell him this as we arrive at my mentor's classroom. He swipes his ID card on the panel beside the door and turns towards me. With a hand resting on the door handle, he pauses and looks like he's about to say something, before the handle is pulled free from his grasp, as someone opens it from the other side.

Jed stumbles slightly but manages to catch himself from

ending up sprawled on the wooden floor. He beats a rather hasty retreat with only an apologetic smile as a farewell. Turning, I look to see who's opened the door and see none other than Mr Fischer.

Well, darn.

CHAPTER 3

Mr Fischer glares down at me and then moves to the side to allow me into the room. I quickly shoot a glance behind me at Jed's rapidly retreating back, no chance of a rescue there, and step into the room. My eyes are instantly drawn to the tall figure standing near the window. He is, quite simply, stunning. No, scratch that, striking. I can't decide, but *wow*. He's well over six feet tall and impressively built. His short dark hair has the reflective quality of a raven's feathers, but it's his eyes that draw me in. They're green, but not in the way most people's eyes are green. These are luminous green. Looking at those eyes, I realise they're also staring intently back at me. Glancing away, I look for a distraction and spy Mr Fischer now standing behind a small desk at the front of the room, glaring at us. I haven't seen him not glare yet, so maybe that's his relaxed face?

"Indigo, this is Kriger. Kriger, this is Indigo. You will be partners for the next two years with me as your mentor. Oh, and please call me Connor. We tend to use first names here."

Kriger and I both turn our attention to Connor as he starts to lay down the law for our time with him.

"You will be punctual, respectful, and not use your powers to cause harm or even to annoy each other. Also, try your best not to get into relationships with people here whilst you're training."

Kriger lets out an indiscreet snort, which elicits a raised eyebrow from Connor. Okay then, good to know where we stand.

"I'm still recovering from the last teenage romance drama I had in my classroom," Connor continues. "I'm not your friend, I'm your teacher, and I'm here to make you the best guardians you can be. You both have shown a lot of promise during the application process, and I can see from the results of your physical assessments..." He glances down at a tablet in his hand, before resuming. "They were unable to complete the strength and speed tests, so that's where we're going to start."

He abruptly tucks the tablet into his bag, slings it over his shoulder and marches towards the door. Glancing back at us and seeing we're not immediately following him, he frowns.

"Grab your bags and let's go. I've got a car downstairs; I'll drive us to the training fields," he says.

I haven't had a chance to put my bag down yet, so I head straight for the door, catching it before it swings shut after Connor's abrupt departure. Yanking it back I turn to hold it open for Kriger, but his hand is already there, cocooning me in his personal space. I feel intimately aware of his presence and an immediate need for my own personal space. Kriger seems to quickly realise this, or maybe he just realises how close he is to me right now because he backs up a pace whilst still grasping the door. Without looking back, I rush to catch up with Connor.

Twenty minutes later, we arrive at what appears to be a deserted farm. Connor informs us the Academy has been gradually buying up any farmland they can, as they've been expanding their training grounds. It seems like the perfect place to let off some steam. There are vehicles of all different sizes, with padded chains for pulling them, down one side of the field.

There's a strong smell of engine oil permeating the warm air, competing with the smell of the freshly cut grass in the next field.

I spy with delight a purpose-built dirt running track, which cuts across several fields; I might actually be able to test how fast I can really go here. I haven't properly tested myself for a few years. Usually I max out whatever test I'm given, and I've grown a lot in that time. This could be interesting. I'm looking forward to pushing everything into this and not having to hold back. My right thigh twitches in anticipation.

Whilst Connor sets up his equipment and Kriger and I warm up, Connor starts to explain why he's been chosen as our mentor. Apparently, his Tk is strong, so this is, essentially, why I was assigned to him. Tk is not the most common skill, so even my limited amount is worth investing their time in. For Kriger, Connor's ability to hold an electrical shield, essentially creating a null space around him that no electrical signals can travel through – handy when trying to hide from satellite surveillance, apparently – will protect him from Kriger's power. It turns out Kriger's slightly alternative skill is that he can electrically shock people, as long as he has a physical connection with them or they're both holding on to the same piece of conducting material.

The relief on Kriger's face when Connor explains this to us is telling. I'm definitely a tad concerned about Kriger's proficiency and level of control with this skill. Also, what kind of heritage gives him those talents? We both have strength and speed, which is common on Evig, so perhaps he's got a parent from there too? I find myself edging slightly away from him, in case he accidentally zaps me should we bump into each other.

Connor also explains that his other talent is discerning truths from lies. He doesn't fully explain how it works, only that he'll always be able to tell. Something to be wary of, or maybe this is just an underhanded way of making sure we're honest with him? Cassie often says we reveal more about ourselves through our lies. She probably read that in one of her novels.

The first test Connor wants us to complete is the strength test. We work in tandem with each other, pulling nearly identical vehicles along a dirt track. The straps dig painfully into my shoulders, even with the padding the pain is making itself known. By the third vehicle, I know I'm at my limit. I can't quite make it to the end of the track and so admit defeat. Kriger keeps going for two more vehicles before he gives up. One point to Kriger then.

Up next is the racetrack. This is going to be good. I flex my hands trying to rid myself of some of the adrenaline coursing through me. We're to race each other along the track whilst Connor measures our speed with a speed gun. I glance up at Kriger beside me. He looks supremely focused on the distant line of trees; the only sign of tension is a slight tightening around his eyes. I decide to follow his lead and focus on the track in front of us, waiting for the beep from Connor's speed gun.

And we're off.

Kriger makes a far quicker start and is already a few paces ahead. This just drives me to dig in and really push everything I have into this. It works. I start gaining on Kriger and then he's behind me. I hear a slight grunt of frustration and a small smug smile tugs at my lips. The ground is moving incredibly fast beneath me, my feet making little noise whilst I use my toes to propel me forward. The finish line is just ahead.

I cross it and glance behind me at Kriger, who is a good ten paces back. But I'm not looking where I'm going and my foot catches on a small dip in the track. I'm down. Rolling to the side to reduce the impact, I end up on my back looking up at the deep blue sky. Kriger's face blocks the glare from the bright sun as he leans over me.

"Nice landing."

"Thanks," I growl back at him, grabbing his proffered hand. He hoists me up, his hand warm and rough. I'm guessing his preferred weapon is some type of blade too. I notice he has two Rip travel tattoos on his inner wrist: one for Earth and one for Evig. I quickly drop his hand as I realise I'm staring at his wrist as if it'll provide me with all the answers.

"Do you have Evig parentage too?" I ask, my hands now firmly clasped behind my back.

"I'm actually Evigborn, but my mum's from here, so I decided to train here instead."

I'm really surprised. I've never knowingly met someone who grew up on another world before, besides my mother. But now that he mentions it, his accent has been bothering me. It's English, but occasionally he sounds almost French in the way he pronounces some words.

"Wow, okay cool. My mum's Evigborn and my dad is from around here. Although, she died when I was very young, so I never got to ask her much about life back home."

Kriger looks slightly taken aback. I try to dismiss his concern with a wave of my hand; it's unsettling since we barely know each other.

I want to ask him more questions, but Connor's impatience is almost palpable, even though he's on the other end of the track. I also get the distinct impression that Kriger is not up for chatting. "Well, I guess we better run back and see what Connor thinks," I say, and start to jog away, not waiting to see if Kriger follows.

Connor seems genuinely impressed with our results. Well, he's stopped glaring at us for once.

"Not too bad at all. You're well matched, which will definitely help with your training. You can book this facility for private use, so I expect you both to do that. You can still improve, and you'll need to maintain this level of strength and speed, at a bare minimum, if you wish to be considered for one of the better travelling guardian apprenticeships."

There are two types of guardians: static and travelling. Static guardians either work as technical support for the travelling guardians, or they work in OWL immigration. Both types of static guardian jobs come with a certain level of risk, but not as much as the travelling guardian jobs do. Travelling guardians move around the world, to wherever they're needed, and often to other worlds to stop illegal trade or travel. The job often requires them to apprehend people who have challenging skill sets, to say the least.

Everyone who travels through the Rip can only do so with approval from both worlds they're travelling through. The visas they use usually have a time limit and they must report back to the Rip to travel back within the allocated time frame. Unfortunately, some people consider this more of a guideline and need a gentle – but firm – reminder. There are also those who deliberately go on the run.

It's these jobs I'm most interested in. Some people try to smuggle illegal weapons or drugs, whilst others are hiding from their world's law enforcement. Either way, they pose a great risk to the safety of the people on Earth, who I want to protect.

Connor sets us up for our specialist skill practise session, having given us merely three minutes to catch our breath and grab a drink of water. Kriger has to send small electrical charges down metal wires without breaking them, whilst I have to use my Tk to tip an empty aluminium can to the side without letting it fall. He wants to see how long I can hold it in position or, in other words, how long it takes for the pain to be too much. Thank goodness I don't have to cycle home from here; I'm going to need to be still for at least half an hour after this.

I look over at Kriger and Connor whilst they set up. Kriger looks slightly nervous about using his power. It's strange seeing someone who usually appears so confident look a little vulnerable. I can hear Connor mumbling to him in reassuring tones, although they're too far away for me to make out what he's saying.

I decide to leave them to it and work on my problem. I can easily knock this can over, but I'm not confident I can hold it in position, and certainly not for any length of time. Not wanting to have to repeat this, I decide to go all out and see what happens.

Stopwatch in hand, I focus on the can in front of me, letting my surroundings fade into the background, and – using my Tk – give it the gentlest of nudges. It barely wobbles. Trying again, I give it a slightly larger nudge, and it starts to topple. I reach out once more with my Tk and hold it in position. Gritting my teeth, I start the stopwatch. A few seconds tick by and I feel the migraine begin. The tension from my jaw travels to the back of my head and down my neck. It's incredibly painful, and it's getting worse.

After twenty seconds, I can't take the pain anymore and release the can. The sound of it falling over causes Connor to look over at me with a raised eyebrow. The sharp stabbing pain behind my right eye has dulled into a persistent ache, one which will take fifteen minutes to clear. Not wanting to look too weak, I try again. This time I only manage ten seconds before it's too much. On hearing the can again, Connor walks over to me, folds his arms, and audibly sighs.

"Is this really the limit of what you can do?" he asks.

Rubbing my temples, I glance up and nod my head in response.

"Well, I can see I've got my work cut out for me. All I'll say at this point is that even though I have no idea why your Tk causes you this ache, you're better off working through some mild discomfort, rather than having a deadly weapon reach you."

"Mild discomfort?" I respond, incredulous. "This is more than mild."

"As far as I can see, you're still sitting up and talking, so, yes, mild discomfort."

Something about his American accent and commanding tone really makes me picture him in the military. Maybe he did serve at some point. Regardless, I don't have the energy to fight him on this. Instead I place my head between my knees and close my eyes.

Kriger's still working with his wires when Connor gets a call on his phone. He turns his back to us and murmurs into it. He's only on the phone for a minute before hanging up and turning towards us.

"Time to go. I've got things I need to do."

I've been sitting with my head down now for about twenty minutes, and my headache is finally lifting. Kriger and I pack up our stuff and head to the car, where Connor is waiting. He looks slightly anxious and keeps checking his phone. When we arrive, he tells us to both sit in the back as he needs his kit up front with him. No idea what's in his 'kit', and he doesn't offer any answers to my raised eyebrows. Odd.

The drive back is quick and silent. Connor doesn't strike up conversation, and it seems almost rude to start one with Kriger when Connor appears so tense, particularly if something is wrong. I glance over at Kriger to see what he's thinking about Connor's behaviour, but he's staring out of his window and doesn't once glance in my direction.

We arrive back at the Academy and Connor pulls over to let us out. He then drives off without so much as a goodbye. Turning to Kriger, I see him staring after Connor's car with a thoughtful frown upon his face. "I'm going to grab some lunch and have a look around. Catch you later?" I say.

Kriger turns his attention to me. "Huh? Sure, I'm going to go for a run. Still have a lot of energy left to burn after the tests."

"Okay, cool. See you later then."

I turn and head into the building, looking back after a few seconds, but he's already left. No idea where he's going to run around here, as it's challenging to run in the centre of town with all the tourists, and I find it hard to believe he's not already starving. I can't do even a small amount of exercise before needing, at least, a sandwich. Running at full speed today has left me ravenous. Maybe no one will think it's odd if I buy several lunches for myself here.

After stuffing my face full of delicious food, they have seriously good food, it's time to head back to class. We've got induction talks for the rest of the afternoon, but usually it'll be classes in the mornings and mentor training in the afternoons. I'm one of the last people to file through and sit down. Everyone must be keen to get going, so I find myself a seat near the back.

I'm starting to see a few familiar faces now and feel a lot

more relaxed about being here than I was this morning. This talk is about all the classes we'll be taking. As a first year I need to take classes in: other-world languages, policy and cultures, science, ethics, maths, IT, combat training, weapons training and wilderness skills. We also get to pick an elective each term, and there are quite a few to choose from. Those wishing to train as travelling guardians need to select at least one physical elective each year, although we're encouraged to take more, but otherwise it's completely up to us. This term our choices are between skydiving, other-world music, other-world literature, diving, astronomy, programming and other-world cookery. I'm torn between diving and astronomy; I really want astronomy but think I should make my first elective be a physical one to demonstrate I'm putting my all into it.

Unfortunately, the way we're to make our selection is by taking one of the limited number of tickets assigned to each course, which are laid out at the front of the room. If I hadn't gone back up to grab the last donut I'd have been here earlier and sitting closer to the front. I let out a large sigh and my breath inadvertently ruffles the hair of the person in front of me. Miranda turns around in her seat and gives me a rueful smile.

"Rotten luck, isn't it? I suppose it's a subtle way to reward the keen beans down front."

"Possibly, but I wouldn't be surprised if this is some secret test to uncover personality traits that didn't come up in our applications. Or they suck at organising," I reply.

Miranda is still facing me, and I manage to get another quick look at the tiny intricate tattoos on her two index fingers. "What do those tattoos mean, if that's okay to ask?"

She glances down at her fingers and then holds them up for me to have a look. One is the outline of Scotland; the other is a hummingbird.

"They're just personal reminders of who I am, sometimes… I need the reminder."

I lean in closer and ask, "Does that have something to do with your mimicking skill?"

She looks at me as if I've just hit her. "Oh gosh, I'm sorry. I didn't mean to offend you. I've never heard of a mimic before so don't really know what it means."

"No, it's okay, I don't really like to talk about it though. But, essentially, yes, it's one of the main reasons why I have these." She wriggles her fingers, then turns around to face the front, as the teacher is talking again.

I'm quite thankful for the interruption. I've really got to work on knowing when to stop prying into people's personal business. I'm a helplessly nosey person, perhaps even more so than Cassie. We were a bit of a handful back at school, often poking our noses in where they weren't wanted. We did once discover the school canteen was mislabelling its supposedly vegetarian options. We felt like proper investigators then, even though it was a relatively small discovery.

I miss her. It doesn't feel right doing all of this without her here with me. I even miss her constant, breathless chatter. A wave of homesickness washes over me. I'm not even far away from home, but Cassie is part of my home life. She's a sister in all but one sense of the word, and this is the first time I can remember being without her.

People are suddenly stuffing their belongings into their bags and moving swiftly to the front of the room, and I realise they must have made the announcement to select our electives for this term. By the time I make it down, there are only a few tickets left, but, thankfully, one of those is for astronomy.

I decide to cycle home via the training ground. I really want to have another go on the running track. Although I haven't booked it, I can't imagine anyone using it right now because it's getting dark. It's only slightly out of the way, and as I can use the cycle paths, it takes me a short half an hour to get there.

The firmly locked outer gates block my path. There are lights shining down on them, as if to highlight my stupidity, and everything else is blanketed in darkness. I decide I don't want to run in the dark anymore – although I had planned on using my bike light. There's something foreboding about this place in the evening. I can't even see where to scan my ID card, and I certainly don't want to break in, so I start backing up.

Out of the corner of my eye, I sense movement. It catches my attention and I swiftly turn my head to see what it is. A moving shadow and a flash of light from a torch have me scurrying behind a nearby bush, dragging my bike with me. I'm not sure why I'm hiding, but the locked gates make me feel like I'm not allowed to be here.

The torch light pauses and swings my way. I hold my breath, hoping whoever this is thinks it's just an animal passing. The invading light eventually retreats, and I can see the person has now placed the torch on the ground to light their way.

They appear to be moving boxes out of their car and into the barn. I can't see who it is or what those boxes are, but I think it's a man and those boxes look seriously heavy. I don't want to make any further noise, so decide to wait in my hiding spot until they leave and I can go home.

I don't have to wait long before the man finishes unloading

his car and heads my way. He drives up to the gates and stops to get out of his car. The interior light comes on. It's Connor. I relax slightly at the sight of him; he's likely just unloading equipment for the Academy. I feel myself tense up again at the tone of his voice when he answers his phone.

"I'm leaving now… I think I got all of it. No, no one saw me at either location. For goodness' sake, Merk, calm down… We got there in time… Just get this stuff out of here and back to Evig as fast as you can… Right, bye."

Connor gets out of his car to unlock the gates and leaves, locking them behind him. I wait until I can no longer see the lights from his car before leaving my hiding place.

This is seriously strange. The conversation did not sound like one an Academy tutor, or even a working guardian, would have. He sounded tense and a little worried, and who on earth is Merk? As far as I'm aware, there are no staff members called Merk, and I haven't come across the name before. The mention of Evig is also suspicious; it's very hard to move much luggage between worlds, and it's meticulously checked. I really need to see what's in those boxes.

Not wanting to wait and get caught by this Merk guy, I decide to jump the fence and take a quick peek. It's probably incredibly stupid, which is why I decide not to dwell on it. There are no obvious security cameras, so I pull the neck of my jumper over my face, just in case, and approach the fence to the side of the gates.

The advantage of increased strength and speed is the ability to jump high. I can't clear the fence in one go, but I'm over it in a couple of seconds, and then running low towards the barn. I quickly reach the barn and slip inside. Thankfully, Connor left the barn doors open, as there's no way I could have opened those old, rusty things without making a racket.

I reach for my phone and angle the light from it towards the floor, so I don't alert anyone to my presence. I head towards the nearest pile of boxes and shine my light on them. They are covered in hazard symbols, many of which I don't recognise, but I think skulls and crossbones are a fairly universal symbol for 'bad'. Not to mention the ones depicting fire. I really don't want to touch these. I look around at the others and see they're all the same. It's definitely time to leave.

I turn off my light and feel my way to the barn doors and head out into the night. Jumping over the fence I get back on my bike, thankfully the slither of light remaining in the sky allows me to see without my bike light. I decide to leave it off until I'm well away from this area. I'm probably being overly cautious, but I'm a tad spooked and want to get home. I'll try and figure all this out soon.

Later that evening, I'm sitting in my house, phone firmly pressed to my ear as Cassie and I unload about our first days to each other. Cassie seems really happy. Her first day at college went well, and she's even joined the LGBTQ+ society there. I can't help but think one of the main reasons she's settled in so well is because I'm not there.

"I can hear you thinking down the phone, Indie. Me having a good day has got nothing to do with your absence. College is just bigger. Those people who might have given us trouble are in the minority here and so won't speak out."

It's spooky how she can read me like that.

"I'm really glad for you, Cass. It's so lovely to hear you sound so happy and relaxed. It was actually really strange how at ease everyone was with each other at the Academy today. I don't think I really noticed it at the time as there was so much to take in, but whenever I discussed my talents or heritage, no one looked afraid."

"That's great! Okay, I want to hear everything, and I mean everything."

"You know I can't tell you everything, the NDA won't allow it."

"Well… okay, no names or places, but tell me everything you can."

I tell Cassie all about meeting Ivy and my classmates. I can't discuss Kriger's name or powers, so instead I just tell her my impressions of him. Essentially, I think he looks the part of a guardian, but his backstory is unusual and he's potentially very irritating. This seems to stoke Cassie's interest, something about the tone of her voice lets me know I'll be getting regular questions about Kriger. I want to tell her about what I found on my way home, but it would almost certainly break the rules of our non-disclosure agreement, so I keep it to myself.

After half an hour of chatting to Cassie, I call time and say goodbye. I'm completely exhausted and just want to sleep. Dad should be home soon, and hopefully he'll be up for cooking supper. I really don't have the energy for negotiating our dodgy stove.

With that thought, I lie back on the sofa and feel the inevitable pull of my eyelids as they close. My mind doesn't seem to want to wind down though and I can't stop picturing Connor as he talks on the phone to the mysterious Merk. What is he up to? Should I tell someone? I don't want to drop my mentor in it after one day, particularly as I don't know much, and it could well be something guardian-related I'm not to know about yet. Perhaps I'd be ruining an undercover operation by speaking out. Also, I imagine the boxes have now been moved, so there won't be anything to corroborate my story.

I don't know who to trust at the Academy yet, so I decide to wait until I get to know someone well enough to tell them. Perhaps Kriger will become that person, but his reaction to Connor's driving off and leaving us was strange, and his sudden need for a 'run' was odd too. I'm almost certainly overthinking this, as I often do, but I can't seem to shake this feeling of unease. Instead, I focus on what Dad and I will eat tonight, as there's no way I'm sleeping without food.

CHAPTER 4

I'm lost, again. I've been at the Luenn Academy for a few days now and finally have my first astronomy lesson, but I can't find the room. It takes me a solid five minutes of negotiating several corridors and staircases, asking different people and getting inconsistent directions, but I do eventually find it.

It's a small classroom, rather than one of the usual lecture theatres, and it feels a little like we're back in school. Our teacher, Ms Fram Hayes, is really stunning, but has the same unyielding expression that Connor has, and so is a little intimidating too. She's an inch or two taller than me, has dark skin and wears her hair in one long braid down her back. Although she looks stern, her voice is kind and jovial. She even discusses her talents right off the bat, which is very refreshing. Her main talents are speed and the ability to manipulate fire, her minor talent is premonition.

"So, in answer to your inevitable questions, yes, I carry a lighter with me at all times, and, no, I cannot accurately predict your future. Now to today's lesson. We're going to have night-time sessions with the telescopes in a few weeks, so we'll look at how they work today. But first I want to discuss what you already know about how our universe compares to others. Specifically, with regards to what we can see when we look up."

She starts to look around the room, and her eyes settle on

me.

"You're Indigo, right? Connor's new charge?"

"Yes, Ms Hayes," I reply, slightly taken aback that my name is already known.

"Great, although please can you all call me Fram? Ms Hayes is my lovely, but slightly terrifying, mother. So, Indigo, what are the main differences people will notice when looking at the night skies on different worlds?"

"Well…" I start. This is a topic I love to talk about. "I've heard of some with more than one moon, and some with no moon at all. There are even worlds where they have colonized other planets in their solar system, and so there is a lot of traffic visible in their skies. Not to mention those that have permanent space stations much larger than ours, or ones from visitors from deep space who are alien to their world."

"Thank you, Indigo." She gives me a small smile, then turns to speak to the rest of the class. "As many of you know, all of these worlds have the potential to have skies vastly different to our own. Due to the chaotic nature of the formation of the planets, particularly how the asteroid strikes affect their development, the planets can change dramatically over time. There is also, as Indigo mentioned, some alien life on a number of worlds, although we haven't been able to find any of our own yet."

"Why is it many other worlds have made contact with alien races?" a voice from the back asks.

I turn to see who it is, but don't recognise the girl with the short dark hair in a pixie cut. Her attention is completely focused on Fram.

"Well, in a few cases it's because life on their world developed faster than it did on our own, and so they were exploring space centuries before us. But in most cases it's because the alien worlds developed millennia before theirs, meaning they can travel vast distances to make contact. It is, of course, because of this contact, often early in the other worlds' development, that mixing of the species has resulted in many of our talents.

"Most of us here are children or grandchildren of someone from another world and likely have alien DNA too. The common saying 'we are all made of stars', although true, means even more to us. The stars we are made from spread across many different universes. Each one of us is unique, some might say special, but remember special doesn't mean better. We are people and we are flawed, we make mistakes and must accept that, for ourselves and for others."

The room falls silent, our gazes fixed on Fram.

"Ahem… well. Sorry, guys. Went off on one then. Back to this lesson. I'd like you to choose a world to research for next week. Specifically, I'd like you to discuss the differences in its night sky, and why those differences exist. Please don't pick a world that you already have a connection to. There are hundreds to choose from. I want you to spend some time thoroughly researching a world that you don't have preconceived notions about."

Fram pings a document to our tablets. Mine vibrates in my bag. Getting it out, I see the outline of the task and some suggested links for us to use to kickstart our work. I scan through the list of worlds but decide to let fate choose for me and pick one at random: Malam. Perfect. I know next to nothing about Malam, except that it's the origin of some people's telepathy. This will be interesting.

I only get to devote half an hour in class to researching Malam, after a brief session on the use of telescopes, before it's time to pack up. All I could glean from my early research is that

Malam is a world of deserts. Its major cities are socially divided between those who have the talent of telepathy and those who do not. Their world's resources have been depleted by alien invasions, in exchange for gifts that advance the more fortunate.

Many parts of their world are mechanised and a lot of their wildlife is actually fake and mechanical. I watched a short video of a mechanical butterfly. It's really beautiful, but also a little unsettling.

Their night sky is quite distinctive, as they have numerous large satellites around their world in a grid-like pattern. I've never seen this before but will be investigating it later tonight.

We all file out of the classroom and grab some lunch before our mentor training sessions this afternoon. I spy Kriger sitting at a table by himself with a very large pasta salad in front of him. All the other tables are occupied, and not knowing anyone else around, I head over. "Mind if I sit?"

Kriger reluctantly looks up with mild surprise from the book he's reading. "Sure." He shrugs. "Fine with me."

"How was your first skydiving lesson?" I ask politely.

"Pretty good, actually. We have to read this book before next time so…"

His attention returns to said book, and I see it's about skydiving in different atmospheres. The title is *Diving and Surviving*. My eyes roll before I can help myself, but Kriger is too engrossed in what he's reading to notice. I don't mind the silence, it gives me time to focus on my food. A cheese toastie, obviously, with fries and a salad. Not to mention two chocolate bars, in case I'm still hungry – I'll definitely still be hungry.

The buzz of the café in the Academy fades to a hum as I zero in on my meal. I glance up a couple of times at Kriger to see if he's put the book down, but he hasn't. He's reading it incredibly fast, from what I can gather by watching his eyes track the lines of text. His lips are slightly pouted in thought, when not chewing, but my attention is drawn to his perfectly arched eyebrows. I realise they're probably not his most impressive feature, but they're so elegant and give him a slightly aristocratic look that's somewhat at odds with his larger build, but it works for him.

My mind wanders back to seeing Connor unload the boxes a few days ago. I've mostly pushed the incident to the back of my mind because I was starting to get paranoid about everyone. I'm not yet comfortable enough with anyone to discuss it, especially not Kriger. I've decided it's best to leave it well alone. It was probably a legitimate guardian mission, and I could get in trouble for being there and witnessing it.

A distant bell rings to let us know it's time for class, and Kriger looks up to catch me staring at his eyebrows. I try to glance away quickly, so he doesn't notice, but I don't think I'm very convincing. He just huffs and gathers his things.

"Shall we head?"

"Sure," I reply, and collect my things too.

We head over to Connor's tutor room, where we've spent the past few sessions working through operational theory. If I'm honest, they've not been the most riveting hours of my life. It's important stuff, of course, and knowing what we should do in certain situations is all well and good, but we need to put this stuff into practise if we're going to have a chance of successfully implementing it. Having sat through lessons all morning, I really want to get moving. If this is another sitting session, I'm going to book one of the training fields to let off some steam.

We arrive at our classroom door to find a piece of paper taped to it reading 'K and I, come and meet me in gym 4 now Be dressed to move. C'.

"Well, isn't he one with words," I remark.

Kriger just shrugs his shoulders and heads off to change. Okay then. Clearly, he's not one for chatting, even without a book to distract him.

I run down to the women's changing room and get into my all-black gear. Black leggings, sleeveless top and my black dancing trainers. I'd rather my boots, but if Connor wants me to demonstrate some martial arts skills, then these won't actually hurt my opponent.

I enter gym four to find Connor and Kriger waiting for me. I sense a slight tension in the room between the two of them, as if they've just broken off a conversation. Yeah, this isn't awkward at all. But then I notice what's also in the room: a large area laid out with crash mats, whilst the rest of the room is curtained off. This is more like it. It looks like I might even get to take Kriger on, or maybe Connor?

"Alright, you two, get yourselves warmed up and then we're going to work through what you already know from your previous training. Hopefully you'll be at a similar level, so you can spar safely with each other."

After a quick warm up, I'm facing Connor. My legs are bent slightly, right foot in front of the left, fists raised up to my cheeks. I'm ready to fight. Connor makes the first move: a jab to my right side, an easy one to dodge, and I follow up with one of my own. We dance around each other like this until he pulls a move I've not come across before, and I'm down. I'm not quite sure what happened. I can usually evade most things due to my speed, but he lured me into an attack, and whilst I was focused on my move, he knocked me down and pinned me.

"Good, your moves are precise and you don't take silly risks. But you need to work on your tactics. Kriger, you're up next."

I watch as Kriger and Connor spar with each other. It really is quite something. Their movements are fluid and fast. I see Connor trying the same move on Kriger that he did on me, but Kriger doesn't fall for it. Instead, it looks like Kriger is about to pin Connor, but as Connor allows Kriger to think he's going down he uses Kriger's momentum to launch himself under and over him and pins Kriger instead.

"Not too bad either," Connor says. "You both have a similar skill level, and when you train with each other you should focus on your speed. It's a real advantage, more so than your strength, but by training together you won't be able to solely rely on it. So, let's see it."

Kriger and I are now facing each other. He's taller than Connor, taller than anyone I've trained with before, and I suddenly feel very small. It's not something I'm used to, and I don't think I like it much either. Whilst I'm pondering the implications of my reduced stature, Kriger makes the first move.

We really are very well-matched. Half my attention is on his shoulders whilst the other half is on his thighs, looking for any indication about what his next move will be. I can see he's doing the same with me. We move around each other for a few minutes before I start to increase the pace, taking a few quick jabs , which he dodges, before retreating. Kriger is the next one to increase the speed with a few kicks to my side. He manages to get one in before I'm away. The kick has knocked my confidence a little and I start to second guess myself, which is when I lose enough concentration for him to swipe my legs out from under me and pin me down.

The weight of his body pushes me firmly into the mat. I can feel the heat radiating off him in waves, and the smell of his soap and sweat infiltrates my nostrils. I shove him off me and can't help but growl at him a little.

Kriger just laughs. "Again?"

I manage to pin Kriger in the next round, which seems to surprise him. Maybe he's not used to being beaten by a girl? But then he wins the next fight.

"Time out," calls Connor. "Go and get some water. Your next session will be in five minutes." Next session? As in another round of combat? I don't really mind as I'm not winded, but I will be a walking bruise tomorrow if we keep it up. However, as we go and grab some water, I see Connor take some equipment out of a back cupboard and then carry it behind the curtained off area of the room.

Kriger and I, having finished our water, head towards Connor and peer around the curtain. We find the rest of the room lined with wooden partitions at various angles with seemingly random cut-outs and raised platforms at different heights linking these partitions. It looks awesome, a bit like an assault course. Connor then chucks two skin-tight black jackets at us to put on, along with black headbands, and bands to go around our legs.

"These are sensors for the laser guns," he explains. "Each band and the entire jacket have sensors throughout, which will detect laser fire. It'll buzz, and your jacket will flash red if it's a kill shot, or it'll vibrate quietly if you're injured. If that happens, you're to remain still and quiet until it stops. The idea here is to apprehend your partner. You can do this without using your weapon, or you can maim them with your gun and then capture them whilst they're down. I'm not giving you handcuffs for this exercise, so holding your opponent's hands behind their back will be sufficient."

"So, it's laser tag?" I ask.

Connor sighs. "Indigo, it's a little more professional than that, but, essentially, yes, it uses similar equipment, although the object of the activity is not the same." He gives us each a small handheld laser gun and dims the lights. "For it not to be completely obvious where you both are, I'll play some music through the speakers, whilst I observe your movements from the cameras in the other room. You have two minutes to find your starting positions. When the music starts, it's go time."

'Go time'? I feel like Connor is trying to make this sound more serious than it is. It's a game. A game I'm completely on board with, however, so 'go time' it is.

I head to the back corner of the room. Although there are no lights on, there's enough light seeping through the large curtain to see by. I can hear Kriger heading to the other corner, or at least I think I do, I'm not entirely sure. I believe my best strategy here is to stay high, that'll make it harder for him to sneak up behind me. I find a platform around eight feet off the ground, jump, pull myself up, and wait.

The music starts, and a tiny near-silent snort escapes my lips as I hear the theme tune to *Guardians Beyond the Rip*, a ridiculous 1980s programme about a small team of guardians working in the north of England. I keep myself perfectly still, so I don't give anything away, and watch for movement.

Nothing. Clearly Kriger has the same plan. Although I really don't want to get captured, I also want to prove myself and beat Kriger. With that in mind, I map out a route from what I can see of the surrounding platforms. The first one is four feet away, an easy jump to make, but perhaps not when I'm trying to stay quiet. I holster the laser gun through one of my thigh sensors, leaving my hands free for balance, and leap. I land through my feet and bend my knees to reduce the noise, but it's not completely silent. Kriger will likely have heard something, although it won't have been easy over the din of the music.

I keep absolutely still and wait for his move.

There, around twelve feet in front of me, I spot him, but he's on the ground moving fast. I decide to take a risk. He probably knows I'm up high, if he heard me before, so I'm going to jump down and wait for him – hopefully catching him by surprise. I glance down to check that the coast is clear and make my move. I land silently, the softer wooden floor absorbing any sound I make.

Hands whip around me and pin mine behind my back. "Darn it! Kriger! I thought I had you."

"Ha! I know, I can't believe you fell for that."

He lets go of my wrists and I rub them vigorously, not because they're sore, more because I'm mad. Mad at myself.

"Indigo, don't be so impulsive," Connor calls from the speaker, where he's turned the music down. "You need to assume your opponent is always a step ahead of you. This is a situation where you need to overthink it. It could be your only opportunity to apprehend someone, and you don't want to waste it."

I nod my head in response, as I know he can see me, and throw a glare at Kriger, who just smiles smugly back.

"Again," Connor calls.

The music slowly increases in volume, and Kriger and I run from each other, ready to begin.

After another hour of training, Connor eventually ends the session and sends us to get cleaned up. I did manage to get Kriger a couple of times, but I was certainly not the winner overall. It's so frustrating. I'm faster than him, not to mention smaller and lighter, so this should have been a walk in the park.

He's clearly had better training than me, or at least more of it. I decide to chat to him about it at the next opportunity. More to make myself feel a bit better, but also because I don't know him very well yet, and we're going to be training together for two years.

I head off to get changed, but my mind is focused on Kriger. He says he grew up on Evig, but he's training here, so which side of the Rip is he going to work on? Is it also not really strange living with his mother's side of the family, who he may not be close to? Maybe he grew up on Evig but has regularly travelled here. I also want to get his take on Connor and whether he thinks he's someone we can trust.

Half an hour later and I still have all these questions swimming around in my head, trying to fight each other to the surface, when I spot the person who can answer them. Kriger is a few paces ahead of me, exiting the building to the front. I run up to meet him at the door.

"Hey, Kriger."

"Oh, hey." He turns slightly and holds the door open so we can both get through. I walk around him and head outside. The late autumn sunshine warms the back of my neck as I turn to face him. I look up into those impossibly green eyes, and realise I have no idea how to start this conversation. So, true to form, I just blurt it out.

"Why are you training here and not on Evig? I mean, are you planning on working here after, or can you do that back home? Not that it matters or anything, I'm just curious." Kriger's eyebrows immediately start climbing their way up his forehead.

"Well, you don't hold anything back, do you?"

"I thought you would've already figured that out from training," I reply with a small smile playing on my lips. Wait, am I flirting with him? I really don't want to be flirting with him.

Kriger huffs a small laugh, but then his face turns serious, and a little wary as we start to walk away from campus together.

"I actually spent a lot of time here growing up," he explains. "Whenever my brother and I weren't in school, we were back here visiting. Both my parents are musicians, along with my brother Lys. It's their thing, their passion. Although I share some of their love for music, I really don't share their talent," he snorts quietly.

This is the first time I've seen an open and honest side to him. I can feel it drawing me in. I think he's left a lot out though, like how he must feel about being the only one in his immediate family who isn't a musician.

"So, what happened?"

"Nothing dramatic. They're often away performing, so I thought it'd be nice to train somewhere near family. My talents actually come from my father's side of the family, although he didn't inherit any of it, but my uncle Merk and I are very similar. Otherwise, I'd think I was adopted."

My heart almost stops at the mention of Merk's name. Kriger turns to look at me when he realises I've gone all quiet. Better say something here, otherwise this is going to get really awkward. "Your uncle?" I reply. Wow, now I sound either suspicious or stupid.

"Yeah, although, I don't really know him very well and haven't seen him in a while," Kriger hastily replies. "I've got to head to my aunt's house now, so, catch you later?"

"Um, sure, yeah, catch you later."

I watch as Kriger picks up the pace and practically speed walks away from me. That was weird. If I wasn't suspicious of

Kriger before, I am now. I don't think I should chat to him about Connor anytime soon, unless things change. Maybe I should speak to someone about Kriger.

This is all so bizarre. There can't be many Merks around here, can there? I mean, I'm sure there's more than one around, but this is quite a coincidence. Kriger seemed to quickly remove his uncle from his life, once he realised he'd mentioned him, almost as if he's meant to keep that part of his life secret. I don't really doubt his story, as it really did sound genuine, or at least the emotion in his voice did. I could do an internet search, but don't want to search any of these names in our network because if anyone is watching, it'll be flagged immediately. I may be paranoid, but those boxes in the barn looked seriously dangerous, so it's likely the people involved will be dangerous too. Best to keep my ears and eyes open, and if I manage to get any more information, then I'll take it straight up to the head of the Academy, Ivy.

CHAPTER 5

It's finally Friday, I've nearly finished my first term and I'm very much looking forward to the weekend and spending time with Cassie. We haven't been able to meet up for a whole month, or even talk, and I really miss her. I can't tell her much about what's been happening, but I really need a friend. Maybe there's a way to discuss what I've found out in some sort of code, so I don't break the NDA?

This morning's lecture is completely full of year one students. All we know is there's to be a big announcement about our upcoming classes that will affect the travelling and static guardian students. There's a certain buzz in the atmosphere today; we're all pretty certain they're going to declare a trip up north. The Rip is located in a smallish town south of Edinburgh, in Scotland. I've never actually been to Scotland before. Dad always wanted to stay well away from anything to do with the Rip. However, he did compromise by living next to the Academy, as we'd already built our lives here before Mum died.

Connor walks through the side door near the front of the lecture theatre and turns to face us. "Morning, everyone. I'm sure you're all keen to hear what we've got planned for you, so I'll get right to it. We've decided to bring our annual trip to the Rip forward this year. Usually, you'd be working with your mentors for a little longer before heading up. However, with the Cross-World Council Meeting happening in a few months, security will be very tight, and they won't allow us to head through the Rip. As this meeting only happens once every five years, it's a prime target for terrorism, so this will also be the focus for our second task up in Scotland." Connor pauses and reaches behind him to set up the large screen.

I feel my tablet vibrate in my bag on the floor and reach down to get it out. Then I notice everyone around me doing the same. I catch the eye of the girl next to me, who gives me a small smile, as we open up the documents sent to us.

The girl leans over and whispers, "I can't believe they're willing to send us up so soon. Why not wait until well after the meeting?"

"Actually, yeah, you're right. This is odd. Maybe there's some other event that happens afterwards? They're so secretive about this stuff, but who knows, maybe we'll actually be able to find out more once we're qualified. I'm Indigo, by the way." I offer her my hand, which she grasps firmly.

"I'm Rebecca, nice to meet you."

Rebecca is on the short side, with long brown hair falling in waves down her back, and clear hazel eyes. We look through the documents together, which appear to be a series of maps and contracts for us to assign our fingerprints to, giving us permission to cross the Rip. Security is so strict, I'm sure this will be just one of the many hoops we have to jump through.

Connor continues his lecture, talking about what documents we'll need to make sure are up to date, before getting onto what we'll actually be doing.

"So, our trip through to Evig will be brief. We'll be allowed into one of their tourist museums and then we'll take a very brief bus ride around the surrounding area. You will not be allowed to get off this bus to do any exploring. As most of Evig is under glass, due to the population's sensitivity to light, this won't be as restrictive as it sounds. However, you are under strict instructions to stay with your assigned guide and to be respectful towards those you meet.

"As for the task once we return from Evig, I can only give you an outline here as you won't be allowed the details until the last minute. So, this will be as close to a real-life scenario as possible.

"You'll be working in teams of four, consisting of two travelling and two static guardian trainees. You'll be given a scenario, perhaps to apprehend a traveller, and you'll need to work together to solve it. These assignments will be in the field, so there will be real-life civilians unaware of what you're doing, and you may well need to camp outdoors as this can take some time.

"I'm not going to answer any of your questions now, as you can save those for your mentor, but know we take this very seriously, and it's a pass or fail assignment." Connor nods sharply and leaves us with that message of impending doom.

There is a collective pause amongst all of us until the room erupts in chatter.

I turn to Rebecca to see what she makes of it all. "Intense, right?"

"Yeah, definitely," she replies. "I can't believe we're to do this so soon after starting at the Academy. We've only got a couple of weeks to prepare."

"Hmm…" I glance down at our updated schedule for the day. "It explains why they now have 'Map Reading' as our next lecture."

"You're right, and look here." Rebecca holds up her tablet screen. "They've brought forward the weapons training too."

"Well, that one I can get behind."

"Definitely," Rebecca says with a grin.

I grin right back at her. I suddenly feel like I've found my friend, someone who's a little bit like me, who I don't need to constantly explain my thought processes to. An immediate sense of calm and relief fills me; I hadn't realised how much I needed this connection until I found it.

The next two hours pass relatively quickly. We have a couple of lectures on map reading and hazard spotting, which is really about how to keep the public safe during operations. Rebecca and I then head off to weapons training together. We've taken every opportunity so far to chat, mostly about growing up amongst people without OWL DNA. She's from Devon, in the south of England, and has just one talent: exceptional eyesight. This didn't sound particularly great, until she explained how she can read small text at incredible distances, and it also makes her an excellent shot.

We arrive at the training room and head inside. We're immediately divided up into pairs – Rebecca and I grab at each other, so we can stay together – and lined up along the far wall.

A small, well-built woman, who I guess to be in her fifties, walks down the line in front of us. Her hands firmly clasped behind her back, she thumps the heels of her black leather boots as she walks. The sound of them makes me think we're about to start boot camp.

"Morning, troops," she says.

Yep, definitely seems like boot camp.

"My name is Dr Brently, but you will call me Chief." She pauses and turns to look at us expectantly.

There's a collective intake of breath before we all respond, "Yes, Chief." Some responses are a tad more forceful than others.

Nodding her head slightly, she resumes her pacing. "My job here is to make sure you know how to safely use all the weapons you will likely encounter throughout your time as guardians. You will then specialise in three." She raises three fingers on her right hand. "These three will require different levels of technology. For, as you know, you will not be allowed the use of any modern technology in some of the worlds."

I'm starting to feel a tad nauseous watching her pace up and down.

"First up, you will watch me demonstrate the three weapons we will work through today: the longbow, handgun and throwing knives."

My heart rate increases at the mention of the knives. I haven't had a chance to practise throwing mine for a few weeks, and I can feel my fingers twitch with excitement. I'm ready to test them out.

"Now, watch and listen closely, but stay where you are. I will only explain each weapon once, and I don't want anyone getting in my way."

We all stay perfectly still. I'm not sure about the others, but I have the distinct impression that drawing attention to myself would be a seriously bad idea.

Chief proceeds to talk through each weapon in excessive detail. You'd think we'd all be bored by the end of her demonstration, but, looking around, I can see we're all completely focused on her. She can make the details of bow design sound fascinating, and I'm positively salivating over the array of holsters for the throwing knives.

"Okay, now that you've seen me demonstrate all three, hang

up your ear defenders on the wall behind you, and we'll get you started on the longbow."

Rebecca and I take turns working through the arrows at our station. She is absolutely an excellent shot, as I was expecting. All of hers hit the bullseye, most of mine do too – once I get the hang of holding and aiming the bow. I didn't even attempt to use my Tk this time because I really don't want to deal with a migraine during the handgun rounds, thanks very much.

Next are the throwing knives. Picking one up off the table, I can instantly feel its quality in the perfect way it's balanced. Throwing it into the target is almost effortless and hitting the bullseye nearly a guarantee. Rebecca whistles softly when she sees me toss three in a row. Even the chief seems to notice and wanders over for a closer look.

"Impressive. I take it you have some experience with these?"

"Yeah, I train with them at home. But I'm not nearly as good as Rebecca was with the long bow," I reply, slightly embarrassed about all the attention. Rebecca should definitely have had some singling out for her performance.

"I'm well aware of Rebecca's abilities, and would expect as much. This level of skill with the knives is unprecedented but not unwelcome. Although you can't take them off the premises, for obvious reasons, you are very welcome to book them out for a training session, or to use the blunted ones for combat practise. Feel free to do so." She spins on her heel, lifts her chin up, and stalks off.

The rest of training passes quite quickly. I don't really enjoy the use of the handguns, as they're loud and the bullets travel way too fast for me to manipulate them. Even in a life-or-death situation, I wouldn't be able to dodge these.

Rebecca and I part ways after a quick lunch together. She

happily chatted away whilst I wolfed my lunch down. I would have contributed more to the conversation, but time was limited, and I needed as many calories as possible before training with Connor and Kriger.

I enter Connor's classroom in the afternoon to find the room filled with more people than I was expecting. Kriger and Connor are up front, along with Fram, my astronomy teacher. Nearer the door are two girls I don't know, although I recognise the girl with the pixie cut from astronomy class. She immediately introduces herself before I even have a chance to say hi to anyone.

"Hi, I'm Ashleigh and this is Freya," she points at the small girl beside her.

Freya lifts her eyes up to meet mine, and smiles slightly, although most of her smile is in her eyes. Freya is only about five feet tall, with shoulder length, mousey blonde hair. She doesn't appear to be very athletic and both her look and manner come across as soft and gentle. She's almost certainly not a travelling guardian trainee. Ashleigh, on the other hand, is her polar opposite. She's tall and well built, her dark pixie cut highlighting her angular facial features. It's a strong look, and it really works for her.

After saying hello to both of them, I look to Connor for an explanation about what everyone is doing here.

"Right then. Now we're all here, let's get started," Connor says and grabs his tablet, tapping at it for a few seconds.

I feel my bag on my back vibrate slightly. Everyone reaches to grab their tablets, and we all look through what he's sent. The document opens up and it immediately asks for a password. Our tablets have simultaneous thumbprint and retina recognition, so we never usually need further password protection. We all look at Connor, Fram included, to see if he has the password we need.

"Your password for this mission is 'youallsuck66'. You cannot write this down anywhere, which is why I did my best to make it memorable."

Connor seems particularly grouchy today, perhaps contributing to the inspiration for this password. Fram is frowning at him. She's actually standing pretty close to him now; she must have moved when I was looking at my tablet. Connor glances up at her and shakes his head ever so slightly. If I hadn't been looking at them at that precise moment, I would have missed it. No idea what it means. Maybe they're just very close? Moving the thought to the back of my mind for later, I type in our memorable password and start scanning through the documents.

There are a lot of them. The equipment list alone is two pages long. Thankfully, it looks like most of it is provided by the Academy, but it's up to us to organise it. As I scan through the pages, I notice there is no actual explanation about our mission.

"So, what exactly are we going to be doing then, besides crossing over to Evig for a day?" I ask Connor.

"Your mission will not be disclosed to you until right before you start it. However, what we can say is that you and Kriger will be working with Ashleigh and Freya to complete it. Ashleigh and Freya are training to be static guardians with their mentor, Fram." Connor gestures fairly redundantly, at Fram before continuing, "They'll be providing tech support from a base."

I look up at Kriger to see how he's taking it all in. He looks at me at the same time and excitement crosses his face, echoing how I feel. This is more like the training I've been hoping to do, and I'm guessing Kriger feels the same.

"Okay, so are we to do some team building exercise or something?" Kriger asks, looking like it's the last thing he wants to do.

"Not quite," replies Fram. "You're to conduct a training exercise together tomorrow, working in teams of two, with one static and one travelling trainee. You'll essentially be playing the game Capture the Flag, but what you'll be working on is your ability to communicate your needs to your teammate at the base, and their capability to direct and assist you." Fram hands out maps to the four of us. "Take these and discuss possible routes and pitfalls you may encounter. I've already briefed my two on the equipment they'll have, so they can answer most of your questions. Freya, you'll be working with Indigo, and Ashleigh, you're to work with Kriger."

I'm not sure why, but the pairings do not sit well with me. The flash of delight in Ashleigh's eyes captures my attention. Oh no, please don't tell me I'm jealous!

I don't think I really like Kriger, and I certainly don't trust him, but I can't deny there's a – very slight – attraction there. Kriger's somewhat unusual behaviour with Connor, and his connection to this mysterious Merk, really don't make him seem reliable. As Ashleigh sidles up to Kriger so they can work together, I try to build internal walls to protect and distance myself from this situation. Best way to not get hurt is to not allow yourself to care. I've had limited success with this method in the past, but it's the only defence I have right now, so I'm going with it. Physically and mentally turning my back on the dark-haired duo, I head towards Freya and get to work.

Freya and I spend the next half an hour speaking softly to each other, so Kriger and Ashleigh don't hear, about possible routes through the terrain to where the flag may be, and potential hazards along the way. She has a really calm manner about her and I instantly feel at ease. Although she appeared almost meek in the beginning, I can hear a steely determination in her voice, which fills me with confidence. I learn I'll be wearing a tracker and earpiece to stay in contact with her, and Connor will let me have one weapon of my choosing.

All this talk about action is making me want to get moving. I'm not one to sit and discuss things when I can be outside doing them. I start to fidget and roll my shoulders to try to eliminate the restlessness, then sense Connor's eyes on me.

"I think that's enough for today," he says. "We'll meet tomorrow afternoon for the exercise, but right now I think Indigo and Kriger could use some more physical training."

Thank goodness. It's like he can read my mind, though I really hope he can't.

Cycling home this evening is challenging after a very intensive training session. The muscles in my legs and arms are actually trembling slightly. Not something I usually experience, but Connor put Kriger and I through our paces this afternoon, and I loved it. He'd set up an outdoor obstacle course. High walls, big jumps, projectile dodging, the works. Not only was it incredibly fun and exhilarating, but having a little bit of extra speed on Kriger meant I won every single time. It was glorious. He didn't seem to mind, much. We were both grinning by the end of it, even Connor's mouth was twitching slightly. It was almost enough to make me like him. Trust him, no, but maybe a little bit of like.

I arrive at home happier and a little sweatier than usual. I run into the house and kiss Dad quickly on the top of his head, whilst he sits reading the news on his tablet. "Just gonna take a quick shower before tea. I've got my astronomy class tonight, so I can't stay for too long."

"Hmm?" He looks up from his screen. "Oh yes, that's right, your first stargazing night. Well, at least that sounds safe."

We're back here again, but I'm not going to take the bait. Deciding to leave him to it, I run up and have a shower. Nothing like a bit of hot water and repressed feelings.

Over dinner, Dad seems to relax a little and even starts a conversation about the Academy. Thankfully, due to him signing the NDA, we can talk a little more freely than I can with others.

"Have you made many new friends yet?"

"A few, even a couple I really like. A girl in my lecture this morning, Rebecca, seems like someone I could really get on with. We're all just so busy training with our mentors, there isn't much time to chat."

"How are you getting on with your mentor and your other trainee, he's Kriger, right?"

"Yeah, well remembered. Connor is working us very hard but I'm actually really enjoying our sessions."

Dad nods his head, seeming quite pleased with my answers. I'm guessing the fact that Connor is working us hard reassures him I'm being well trained.

"Kriger's alright, I guess, but I haven't got to know him very well yet. Only thing I've learned so far is he actually grew up on Evig, but his mother is from here, so he decided to train here."

My dad puts down his knife and fork and stares intently at me. "Did you say he's from Evig?"

"Yes, he grew up there."

"Did you mention to him that your mother was from there too?"

"Well, yes, I did. Why shouldn't I? I wouldn't normally bring it up with regular people, but everyone at the Academy has mixed heritage, so it's not a thing." I can sense the tension radiating from my dad as he gears himself up to whatever he's about to say next.

"That wasn't smart of you, Indigo."

I wait for the explanation because I'm currently drawing a blank. He's always encouraged me to keep my heritage quiet, but that was because of the prejudice I experienced. Or at least I think it was.

Dad is now focused on the food in front of him. Clearly, he wants to leave this alone. "Dad, if you don't tell me why you think this is a bad call, then how am I supposed to tell when I can and cannot discuss my heritage with people?"

"Best to not to tell anyone. Safer that way."

"Safer, why? Mum didn't die because she was Evigborn, she died because she got in the way of an escaped convict from another world." Dad studiously avoids my gaze. "That is what happened, right, Dad?"

"It's what I was told."

"But you're not convinced?"

"I…" he sighs and lays down his knife and fork. "I don't really know anything. Elna would never tell me anything about her work, and I got the distinct impression it was safer for all of us if I didn't ask. So, please, don't discuss who your mother was, and certainly not with anyone who has connections to Evig. I can't stop you from becoming a guardian, but you can at least grant me this, so I know you're taking precautions."

He stares at me intently, and I stare back. I don't want to die on this hill though, so I drop my gaze. "Sure, Dad, I'll be careful and keep quiet."

"Good. Now, hurry up and finish your food. You need to leave in a few minutes. I'm off out this evening with a few friends but won't be home late. You'll probably get back before me, so I'll leave the leftovers in the fridge for you to zap in the microwave."

I nod my head, and wolf down the rest of my dinner, knowing I'll be hungry again by the time I get back.

This is the most Dad has ever talked about Mum in a while, but I can see he's done now. Maybe he'll talk about her more tomorrow. I'll keep my fingers crossed, but I won't hold my breath. One thing is for sure, I won't bring up any concerns I have about Connor and Kriger, at least not yet. He'd certainly use them as an excuse to take me out of the Academy.

Having finished my dinner, I grab my bag and helmet, say goodbye to Dad, and head out to astronomy class.

Fram's class this evening is only a fifteen-minute bike ride along well-lit cycle paths. This is very reassuring, given what can happen to people like me when we're outside alone after dark. I arrive at the private parkland we'll be working in, having shown my ID to the security guard. Not sure why there's a security guard here, and not at the other outdoor sites I've been to. Then I see a full array of working telescopes before me. There must be at least twenty of them, all attached to high-end tablets. There's even something that looks a bit like an observatory at the side of the park. All the students are gathered around one of the telescopes with Fram, so I quickly hurry down, only then realising I'm the last to arrive.

"Good, you're here, Indigo. Let's begin."

Fram proceeds to take us through the workings of the telescopes we'll be using. We are to practise using them manually and with the tablets.

I spy Jed standing to the right of Fram, and Ashleigh a few feet from me. Ashleigh catches my eye and gives me a warm smile. I return it, although somewhat reluctantly. As for Jed, he appears to be helping out this evening. As a second year, and former student of Fram's, he's volunteered to assist. He seems to be helping out with a lot of different things at the Academy. I wonder if this is a requirement, or maybe he gets paid?

Fram's instructions are brief but comprehensive, and then we're all working with our own telescopes. It's a skill we're unlikely to get to use in our future careers, but some of us may be lucky enough to be the first future visitors to a new world. Investigating their night sky is a high priority, mostly to spot any obvious differences and to check for space stations. Of course, if we deem it safe for civilians, then scientists can visit and investigate further.

Jed and Fram work their way around all of us, giving each student pointers. Fram is not one to gush with compliments, but I really like how direct she is. She actually has a few more positive things to say when she reaches Ashleigh's station. Ashleigh's a clear whiz when it comes to anything technical. Jed, however, is full of praise. He comes up behind me, waiting patiently for me to finish positioning my telescope through the finderscope mounted on top.

"Can I have a look?"

"Sure," I reply, moving out of the way, careful not to touch him as he moves around me.

"Good work, Indigo, you've lined Saturn up beautifully. If you look through the eyepiece, you'll be able to see its rings and a few of its moons."

I move up next to him, our shoulders brushing as I lean forward to have a look.

"Wow, that's beautiful." I can't believe the level of detail I can see through this one small telescope.

"Yeah, this is a good time of year to view Saturn, and for general stargazing, particularly as it's so flat here." Jed leans back and tilts his head up to look at the stars.

I stand up too and look over at his profile. He seems to have a genuine passion for the night sky. Although I've never used a telescope before, I have often used Dad's binoculars to see what I can find.

"Have you ever done any skygazing on another world?" I ask.

Jed glances down at me, his blue eyes are captivating.

"At the end of my first year, I was lucky to be selected to go on another visit to Evig. Fram took a few of us out in the evening to have a look."

The intensity of his gaze thrills me slightly. I do my best to ignore it.

"Sounds amazing. I've heard their sky is slightly different to our own."

"Hmm, yes, you're right," he replies, returning his gaze to the sky. "Nothing obviously different, unless you know what to look for. You've got family there, right? Maybe you'll be invited over soon and get to look for yourself."

A cool sensation rapidly fills me; I don't remember discussing my heritage with Jed. "How did you know I've got family in Evig?" As far as I'm aware, given my mother was adopted, I don't think there are any family members left on Evig.

Jed glances sharply down at me, his pupils dilating slightly, but then he grins. "Didn't know, just a lucky guess. I mean, your hair and skin colour are a dead giveaway."

"Huh, oh right, sure," I reply, only slightly mollified.

"Anyway, better continue to make the rounds. Nice chatting to you, Indigo." He gives my shoulder a squeeze and moves on.

I can't shake the feeling of unease from chatting with Jed. I'm sure it's merely a coincidence. If I hadn't had the conversation with Dad earlier, I'd not even bat an eyelid. I just don't like coincidences.

The rest of the lesson passes uneventfully and before long, I'm cycling home. The uneasiness I felt in class only intensifies as I head back alone. I can't shake the sensation of being watched. I decide the best thing to do is to pedal fast and get home. At least there I can lock the door and be relatively safe.

I arrive back home in record time, only to find the front door open. Except, it's not just open, it's hanging off its hinges

CHAPTER 6

I walk cautiously into my house. "Dad?" I whisper, not sure if whoever broke in is still here. I don't get a response, so decide not to be an idiot and to do the sensible thing. I call the police, quickly followed by my dad and then Cassie. The police and my father are on their way, but I don't want to hang around outside and wait for them, so I head over to Cassie's instead. Thankfully, she lives one street away, and she's already at the door waiting for me.

"Indie, are you okay, what happened?" she asks, immediately reaching out to hug me.

I return her hug with a squeeze of my own and tell her what I found when I got home.

"Wow, that's super creepy and scary."

Cassie's mum appears behind her wearing the fuzziest pink jumper I have ever seen.

"Come on in out of the cold. Indigo, you hungry?" she asks as she heads towards the kitchen.

"Always," I reply with a small grin. It's good to have a backup home.

In a few short minutes, the three of us are tucking into some jam on toast, four slices for me, when my dad knocks on the door. I'm up and out of my seat in a flash to let him in. He envelops me in a huge hug, which washes away the lingering anxiety I was holding onto. Cassie's mum, Susan, comes up behind me to take the bag of essentials he grabbed for the two of us, and gets us all to sit back down and eat.

"Have the police said anything yet?" I ask.

Dad finishes his mouthful of toast and looks up at me. "Well, the weird thing is, it doesn't look like much, if anything, was taken."

"You mean all our stuff is okay?" Well, this is a stroke of luck, although I have a sneaky suspicion this isn't the good news I was hoping for.

"It seems so, but it does raise the question of why. The police are concerned they were looking for something in particular, but they couldn't verify that. Or, more likely, given we have nothing of value, it's a case of mistaken identity. Chances are our house wasn't the one the burglars were supposed to invade."

"That's good news then. They're unlikely to come back if they didn't take anything this time around, right?" Cassie asks, eyes wide as saucers.

She actually seems more frightened about the burglary than I am. Even Susan, who's clenching her hands around her coffee mug, seems worried. I don't know why I feel almost calm, but once Dad arrived, I knew he would take over the worrying for the two of us. Maybe it's time for me to step up and share some of our burdens.

A short while later I hear my phone buzzing on the countertop and reach over to see who's calling this late. It's a withheld number. Given the weirdness of this evening, I decide to risk it and see who it is.

"Hello?"

"Indigo?"

"Yes, who's this?"

"This is Rose calling from the office of Ivy Jenkins. The Luenn Academy has just received a notification from the police that your house has been broken into. Is that correct?"

"Yes," I respond hesitantly. How have they got this information so quickly?

"Right, we need you to come to Ivy's office first thing tomorrow at 8:00 to discuss this with her."

"Discuss this?"

"Yes, we need to ascertain whether you were targeted because of your affiliations with the Luenn Academy, or if it was a random incident."

"Umm, well the police don't think they took anything, and so they likely burgled the wrong house." I can't believe I'm having this conversation. Why on earth would someone target me because I'm at the Academy?

"Even so, we need to eliminate this as a possibility. Can I put you in the diary for 8:00?"

"Sure, yes, you can do that. I'll be there."

"Thank you, Indigo. Have you and your father secured suitable alternative accommodation for the evening, or do you require assistance?"

"No, we're all set, thanks."

"Good, right then. See you here at 8:00 tomorrow. Goodbye." Without waiting for a reply, she hangs up.

I sit there staring at my phone for a second, with everyone's eyes upon me, waiting for me to speak. All I can think of is how on earth the Academy found out about the break-in so quickly. The Luenn Academy *is* part of a very large organisation, but I'm such a small part of it that it's a little strange for them to pay me special attention. I haven't been in the Academy long, so perhaps this is normal procedure, but I can't help but feel a little unsettled.

"Well?" asks Cassie impatiently. "Or is this something else you can't tell us about?"

Her tone of voice surprises me: it's almost resentful. It's the first time she's said anything in any way negative about me being at the Academy.

"They want me to come in early tomorrow to talk about it. They want to make sure it's not Academy-related, although I've no idea how I can really help with that."

"Hmm," mumbles Dad. "They might actually just want to know whether you had any sensitive information in the house, like in a diary? You don't keep a diary, do you?"

"Ha! Time to write in a diary sounds nice, but no, I don't think I have anything that could connect me to the Academy, apart from my acceptance letters."

"Well, all this talk is not going to help anyone go to sleep," announces Susan. "I suggest we finish up here and retire for the night. Indigo, I'm sure Cassie won't mind you sharing her room. Matthew, you can have the spare room."

"Thank you, Susan," says Dad, running his hand through his light brown hair. "You've been a huge help."

We chat for another half an hour before clearing up and settling in for the night. The light from Cassie's faux candle produces dancing shadows on her bedroom wall.

"Indie?" Cassie asks, once we're both in bed.

"Hmm?"

"Are you okay? I'm sorry I snapped at you downstairs. I'm just frustrated I don't really know anything about your new world, and we haven't been able to meet up for ages."

"I get it." I'm so relieved she's brought this up. I hate when things are tense between us. "I feel the same about your new life too, so can only imagine what it's like when I can't tell you everything. But I can talk in general terms, and it would be really good to talk to you about all this stuff. Particularly because you're not part of the Academy." Maybe I can find a way to talk to her about Connor's weird behaviour, not to mention my dad's warning about telling people about my heritage. Now that I think about it, the connection between our home getting broken into and my heritage being revealed to a couple of people at the Academy is worrying.

"You can tell me anything. Confidential or not, I won't tell anyone."

With a deep intake of breath, I tell Cassie everything. Well, almost everything. I omit names and the specifics of the Academy's training programme. Cassie stays quiet throughout, listening intently. With every word, the tension in my shoulders lessens, and the weight of worry I've been carrying decreases. When I tell her about my latest suspicions about the break-in, she audibly gasps.

"Geez, you might be right. It's some coincidence. I mean, if the burglars actually stole some things, then it'd be easier to write off. With any luck you'll get some answers at your meeting in the morning. It doesn't sound like there was anything for them to find, so, hopefully, if they were connected, there won't be any more break-ins."

"You think? Or maybe they saw some photos of my mum and have now linked me with her. I'm not even sure Dad truly knew what my mum was involved with. Maybe she angered the wrong people with an investigation? Or even found something out that they don't want discussed? I have no real idea what to think anymore. I was so sure Mum's death was an accident, a risk of the job. But now, I don't know what I'm sure about." I can feel myself start to slip back into a worry spiral.

"That kind of thinking will get you nowhere. What you need is a plan. You need to go to the meeting tomorrow, and make sure she answers some of your questions too. Plus, a one-on-one with Ivy should be fun. I know how much you admire her." Cassie starts ticking off her points on her fingers. "Next, you need to investigate your mentor and training partner and see whether either can be trusted."

"Okay. I like the first part of the plan." Just the thought of a plan, even a small one, helps calm my anxiety and allows me to focus on something more positive. "I'm just not sure how to go about the second half."

"Ask around. Not about anything specific, just about other people's general impressions of them."

I don't know why this hasn't occurred to me before. I think I was waiting for divine inspiration to tell me whether they were trustworthy or not. Perhaps not the best method. "Thanks, that sounds like a workable idea,"

"Get some sleep, and work on your plan tomorrow." And I do.

I wake early, feeling restless. I want to get to work on my new plan of action. I think the best way to get rid of this restlessness is to go for a short run around our neighbourhood, which will also give me an opportunity to swing by our house to see if there's been any further activity.

After a few warm-up stretches, I sneak out of the house, taking care not to wake anyone. The cool, fresh air caresses my face, my warm breath condensing in front of me. Running gives me a sense of control. I can't have full control over the situation, but at least I have control over my body.

The streets are empty and quiet this morning. All I can hear is my breathing and the taps of my feet along the pavement. Our front door has been replaced with a makeshift wooden one, which makes it seem less like our house. There's a sense of wrongness about the whole scene. Knowing strangers have been through my things brands the house as tainted, almost dirty. My fingers clench in anticipation of getting rid of the invisible dirt. I don't want to linger here too long, and waste most of this morning's exercise time, so I turn my back on the house and continue my run.

Returning to Cassie's an hour later I find the rest of the household beginning to stir. The smell of coffee coming from the kitchen greets me as I come inside.

"Indigo, is that you?" asks Susan from the kitchen.

"Yes, just going to pop into the shower if that's okay?"

"Of course it is, sweetie, I'll have some breakfast ready when you get down."

I quickly call out a thank you as I run up the stairs.

After a quick breakfast with everyone, and a rather rushed bike ride to the Academy, I make it to Ivy's office just in time. Sitting outside is a woman who appears to be in her thirties, with long auburn hair pulled back tight and impeccably applied makeup. She must have been up early.

"Good morning. Indigo, I presume?" asks Ms Impeccable.

"Umm, yes, that's me." I take it Ivy Jenkins likes things formal.

"Lovely. I'm Rose. We spoke on the phone yesterday."

She pauses, waiting for a response. Having no idea what to say, I just nod. This seems to satisfy her.

She continues, "Ms Jenkins should be ready to receive you now. Please come this way."

I follow Rose around the corner to closed, wooden double doors. She knocks once, opens one of the doors slightly and pokes her head through the gap to announce my presence. I can't hear Ivy's response, but it must have been positive because Rose is now ushering me in.

Ivy Jenkins' office is vast. The lower half of the walls are covered in dark wood panelling, whilst the upper half are painted a calming mint green. The décor is on the older side, slightly at odds with the modern shaped-and-coloured windows of the Academy.

Ivy sits behind her desk in a dark green leather, low-backed chair, her blonde hair swept up into a chignon, and her right hand tapping her pen thoughtfully on the pad in front of her. I stand on the other side of her desk, hands clasped behind my back, and glance over at the door as Rose closes it. I feel like I'm in the military standing to attention, and although the Academy doesn't train us to be soldiers, a lot of what we do is similar.

As I face Ivy, I realise there is no seat for me, nor does she offer me one. Instead, she looks to be assessing my appearance. I glance down at my black denim trousers and burgundy top, checking to see if anything's amiss. Apparently, she seems satisfied, as she gives a short sniff in my direction and then begins her speech.

"I'm sorry to hear about the break-in at your family home last night. Are you and your father okay?"

I nod my head, but before I can properly respond she ploughs on.

"Good, well, what we at the Luenn Academy need to check is whether your home was targeted because of your relationship with us. I obviously don't expect that to be the case. I've read the report from the police, who also believe your house was targeted by mistake, but we need to be sure."

If she was so sure this wasn't to do with the Academy, why on earth is she interviewing me rather than having one of her assistants do it? I don't get much chance to think about this before she starts peppering me with questions.

"Did you make any copies of the documents you signed for us, which we store here?"

"No."

"Is there any chance you misplaced any sensitive information and perhaps forgot to mention this to us?"

"No."

"Do you keep a diary, even one where you don't discuss your training at the Academy?"

"No."

"Does your home have a security system, which perhaps could have recorded you discussing your training with your father?"

"No."

"Is there anything in your house you can think of that might have sensitive information on it linked to the Academy?"

"No."

"Right then. Thank you, Indigo. I understand having your home broken into can be a distressing experience. Do let my assistant, Rose, know if you require any counselling or further help getting your home back up and running."

"Umm, thanks, but I don't think that'll be necessary."

This woman is seriously intense. I've seen her interviewed by people on TV, social media, and, of course, sat through her induction speech, but I wasn't prepared for this kind of interrogation. She seems happy with my answers though.

"Very well, best of luck to you." She turns her attention to the notepad in front of her and starts scribbling.

After a few seconds pass, I realise I've been dismissed and make a hasty exit through the double doors. I pass by Rose's desk and give her a tight smile but don't stop. I feel the need to go and burn off some excess energy. Perhaps hitting something will help. I round a corner and bump into Jed, literally.

After we both disentangle our respective limbs, we jump back to take stock of our belongings. I, thankfully, still have my bag on my shoulder and my jumper in hand, but unfortunately all of Jed's papers are strewn across the hardwood floor.

Without comment, we both bend down and gather them up quickly. I don't get a chance to see what's on them, only that they seem to consist of maps and documents. I straighten up to give him an apologetic smile, but my smile doesn't last long when I notice how uncomfortable Jed appears. He's usually so relaxed and put together, but he seems upset about something and is almost hopping from one foot to the other.

"Sorry, I didn't spot you there. Are you okay? You seem a little jumpy. I don't think I'm that terrifying this early in the morning," I joke, hoping to relax him a little. All this nervous energy is starting to put me on edge.

"It's no problem, I'm just in a rush. I have an appointment with Miss Jenkins."

Ah, okay. "Well, I won't keep you. Hope it's not too serious."

Jed nods slightly as he backs away, before making a hasty turn towards Ivy's office. I don't watch him chat to Rose, instead I decide to make a swift exit myself. I've got an hour to kill before class this morning, so I think the sparring room in the gym is what's called for. They have plenty of reinforced dummies there I can hit.

I quickly change into my workout gear and head to the lower ground floor gym. This space mostly consists of mats for sparring, but there's also a row of dummies lining one side of the room, which have increasing levels of reinforcement depending on your strength. Having been shown this earlier by Connor, I know I need it at max strength, so I don't send it flying.

The room is empty and silent. I decide to forgo my headphones and focus on the sounds and movement of my body instead. I start off with a few gentle jabs and kicks to warm me up before I let go and release all the tension from the past twenty-four hours.

After about ten minutes of pummelling the dummy, I hear the door open and close behind me. I look back to see who it is. Kriger walks in with a towel slung over his shoulder. I give him a small wave before focussing my attention back on the dummy. He gives me a nod and heads to the end of the row, where he chooses a dummy. If I tilt my head slightly, I can see his strong well-built figure trying to punch the stuffing out of his dummy.

After another ten minutes, I'm really working up a sweat. Wiping my brow with my forearm, I look in Kriger's direction to see him removing his T-shirt. I actually stop moving, arm still resting against my forehead as the expanse of tanned, muscular skin is revealed before me. Oh my.

I notice the muscles in his back tense, then relax. Kriger turns around to find me rapidly averting my eyes as I resume punching my dummy. I'm guessing my silence whilst he removed his top was a bit of a giveaway. Cheeks flaming, I concentrate on my workout, pushing my body as much as I can with the minutes remaining.

In what feels like a very short amount of time, my watch

vibrates to remind me to change before class. I lower my hands and turn it off, then see that Kriger is simply standing there, watching me. His mouth is pulled up to one side in a half smile.

"Sorry, you were so in the zone there that I didn't want to interrupt," he says with a small shrug of his broad shoulders.

His top is back on now and there's a faint sheen of sweat coating his arms and face. I think I should be slightly grossed out, but I'm really not.

"Umm, yeah, I guess I was." Smooth, Indigo.

"I wanted to ask," Kriger continues, "if we could chat about something before our training session with Connor this afternoon. Maybe over lunch?"

My stomach betrays me and does a little flip, but from the serious expression on his face, I don't think he wants to talk about anything casual.

"Sure, fine with me. Is anything wrong?"

But as Kriger opens his mouth to answer, there's a distant heart-stopping scream from upstairs.

We both look at each other in shock, before simultaneously breaking into a run to get upstairs and investigate. The sound of the scream has sent more than shivers down my spine, it's made every nerve in my body vibrate in anticipation of a fight. We sprint up the stairs and around the corner to find ourselves in the main foyer. My eyes are immediately drawn to a small cluster of people huddled around someone lying on the floor. We race over, and I land heavily on my knees when I see who's hurt. It's Fram.

Her eyes are closed but her chest is moving, so she's breathing, thank goodness. I look up at those around her and hear someone calling an ambulance.

"What happened?" I ask. Kriger is beside me now, his body

pressed alongside mine as he tries to see what's going on.

"We don't know. I didn't see it happen, but I heard her scream and then the sound of her body hitting the floor," a middle-aged woman with short dark hair answers. "I don't know how she fell. She must have fallen from the first-floor gallery, or at least I hope it was just the first."

The woman starts trembling and a man I recognise from reception puts his arm around her.

Kriger and another woman are checking Fram over for injuries whilst trying to wake her. I hear the pounding of footsteps on the stairs and look up to see Connor racing towards us. His face is ashen. He pushes two people aside to get to Fram.

"Fram, oh no, Fram! Has someone called an ambulance?" Before waiting for a response, he turns his attention back to Fram, shaking her shoulders slightly. "Fram, honey, come on, please wake up."

My eyebrows try to reach my hairline with that revelation, but I can't think on it for long as Fram starts to come around.

"Connor? Why, why am I on the floor?"

"Oh, thank God, Fram. Are you hurt?" Connor's hands start travelling along the sides of her body looking for injuries. "How on earth did you fall from the gallery?"

"I... I didn't fall. I was pushed."

CHAPTER 7

"Pushed! Who pushed you Fram?" Connor's face reflects the sound of urgency in his voice. His hair, which is always so neat, looks ruffled from having run his hand through it so many times.

"I don't know. I… ouch… couldn't see them." Fram manages to sit up with help from Connor. "I had a premonition, right before it happened, to run, but there wasn't any time. Whoever did it, they can't have planned it. Otherwise, I should have had that… ouch, premonition earlier."

Fram is now sitting up and drinking a glass of water that someone gave her. I can see the paramedics coming through the front doors, and it looks like she's going to be okay. Hopefully there aren't any internal injuries.

I had no idea how Fram's power worked. It's possible the person who pushed her knew and spotted an opportunity when walking past. I don't have a chance to ask Fram any questions, as we are all swiftly pushed to one side by the paramedics. Connor stays with her and accompanies her in the ambulance. I knew those two were close. Maybe they're in a relationship?

Kriger nudges my shoulder with his, jolting me out of my thoughts.

"You okay? I don't think there's much we can do here now," he says, looking around him to see if we're needed anywhere.

We overhear security discussing doing a sweep of the upper floors, to look for anyone who might not belong. But since Fram couldn't give a description of her attacker, there's not much they can do until they review the security footage.

"Yeah, I'm okay, apart from being completely freaked out that someone tried to kill Fram, of course." I can hear a slight tremor in my voice. This is supposed to be our safe space, and someone violated it. Having my home broken into last night and now this, I feel very exposed, almost helpless.

I straighten my spine and focus on what needs to be done. Primarily, figuring out what on earth is going on with Connor, and possibly with Fram and Kriger. What better person to speak to than Kriger himself. His genuine concern about Fram is somewhat reassuring, so he's probably not a complete jerk. He said he wanted to chat at lunch, but he won't be the only one asking questions. Feeling a little better already, I walk with Kriger to our respective changing rooms and get ready for class.

When I emerge, the building has filled with students ready to start their day. Amongst them, I spy Kriger waiting for me. He's leaning against the wall opposite, one knee bent, with his boot resting against the whitewashed wall. He cocks his head to one side and I see his eyes give me the once-over before he pushes off the wall and heads towards me.

"I thought you might want some company. I don't like the idea of people wandering around here by themselves right now."

By 'people', I take it he means me? My heart starts beating a little bit faster, coupled with a sense of indignation. I can definitely take care of myself. However, I don't want to shut him down right now, as I want him to be open and honest when we have our chat later. And it's probably the first time he's gone out of his way to be nice to me.

"Thanks, sounds good," I say. "Actually, my house was broken into last night, and now with what happened to Fram, I can't say I'm feeling very relaxed."

Kriger looks at me. "Wait, what? Was anything taken? Were you there when it happened?"

His eyes are full of concern as they rove over my face looking for answers, which surprises me a little.

"No and no, thank goodness. Although having nothing taken does make it a tad more unsettling. I had to come in early to speak to Ivy about it, in case it was Academy-related. That was an interesting experience. I can't decide if I'm terrified of her or if I want to be her. Anyway, she doesn't think it was related, and the police think it was a case of mistaken identity." I lift my eyes up to meet his.

Kriger is looking at me with an unreadable expression, but he doesn't get a chance to reply as we've reached the top of the stairs and are suddenly surrounded by a group of students who immediately start throwing questions at us. They must have gotten wind of what happened with Fram, and knew we were there. We try to answer some of their questions, but we really don't know much, so we can't answer most of them.

Kriger guides me through the throng and into the lecture theatre. For the first time this year, he voluntarily sits down next to me. It's a little strange when he's been so standoffish outside of training. I really hope he doesn't think I'm some sort of damsel in distress. I am definitely *not* one of those.

There's a buzz of chatter in the room as people discuss what happened with Fram. The noise from everyone's voices masks the sound of Ivy entering at the front of the room, and it takes a full minute for everyone to spot her and fall silent. Once she has everyone's attention, there isn't even the rustle of fabric, as we are all so focused on what she's about to say.

"We are all deeply shocked about what happened this morning with Ms Fram Hayes. I have spoken to her doctors and they are confident that she will make a full recovery. She should be back with us next week. We do not fully know the circumstances of her accident, so I would ask you all to refrain from speculation.

"The safety of our staff and students is of the utmost importance to us, so, with that in mind, we will be increasing security on all floors. You will see more security officers as well as increased security checks as you enter the building. Counselling will also be offered to anyone who would find it beneficial. Please get in touch with your tutors, and they will point you in the right direction. I thank you in advance for your support with this. Now," she says, her expression quickly shifting from serious to jovial, "I hear you're all in for a treat this morning. So, I shall pass you on to Ms Beckett for your lecture on maintaining public safety when on a mission." She raises her right arm and welcomes Ms Beckett onto the platform at the front of the room.

I feel a bit sorry for Ms Beckett. Her lecture is certainly important, but I wouldn't have called it a treat. Ivy has managed to shut down most of the rumours about Fram's incident – I refuse to call it an accident – and I have a sneaky suspicion we're not going to hear any more about it. Perhaps they'll use this incident as a reason to further monitor our activities. Or maybe I'm being a tad paranoid?

Ms Beckett's lecture proves to be slightly more engaging than I, and I'm guessing most people in this room, anticipated. She runs us through a few scenarios we may encounter during our assessment, and how to reduce and eliminate risk to the public. Their safety is a fundamental part of our mission, and our future careers, so any additional risk we pose to the public will likely cause us to fail this task.

I'm actually a little anxious about this exercise next week. It seems way too soon for us to be training around the general public. Kriger's talent is particularly hazardous, and although his control has gotten a lot better, he hasn't had much practise in a stressful environment.

I glance up at Kriger and notice the tension in his jaw. Could he be thinking the same thing? He definitely seems riveted by Ms Beckett's lecture; it's encouraging to see my teammate taking this as seriously as I do. We're going to be very reliant on each other, as well as on Ashleigh and Freya, to pass this assessment and stay safe.

The rest of the morning's lectures pass pretty quickly, and already Kriger and I are heading up to have lunch before our mini training mission with Ashleigh and Freya.

"I just realised: do you think we're still doing the training exercise this afternoon if Fram is in hospital?" I ask Kriger.

Kriger actually stops walking. He looks perplexed.

"I hadn't thought about that either, but you're right. Connor might even still be at the hospital." He pauses. "Well, we haven't heard anything, so I guess we head over and see what's happening? Did Freya show you pictures of the site?" His face takes on a look of excitement.

"Yeah, it's a pretty big place. I guess we could always do our own training exercise, if it ends up being just the two of us." Wait, what did I just say? Kriger's breath hitches slightly as he stares at me. "I mean, it's enough space to really stretch our legs and race," I hurriedly add.

Kriger releases his breath and resumes walking up to the

canteen. "Sure, training just the two of us doesn't sound too bad."

Oh God, is he flirting with me? I'm not sure what to think.

We've reached the canteen. Kriger has his back to me whilst he places his order, so he is, thankfully, unaware of my perplexed expression. I'm going to ignore the situation for now. I'm probably misreading it entirely. Instead, I grab a tray and quickly fill it up with carbs and protein. Whether training with Connor is on or not, I'm going to need to eat.

Kriger and I find a secluded table near one of the small circular windows and tuck into our food. I'm glad he wants to eat before our chat because I seriously don't think I could concentrate on what he has to say if there's food waiting in front of me.

We quickly scoff down our lunch, then sit in awkward silence. I don't know what he wants to talk about, so I'm not going to be able to help him out here.

The silence stretches on until it's painfully thin. I start fiddling with the tassels on my hoodie. It's a very nice hoodie. It's dark burgundy, to match my top, with navy blue vertical stripes down the sides and it has a nice slim fit. It takes me a couple of seconds to stop thinking about my jumper and realise Kriger is focused on me.

"Okay, so I need to talk to you about something, and after this morning's events, I think it's really important to lay all my cards out on the table."

He looks nervous. His hands are clasped firmly in front of him and he's leaning forward with his elbows resting on the table.

"Okay," I reply warily. "You're definitely starting to worry me now." I'm not sure if this is going to be a revelation about his personal life or if he's about to tell me he's a spy.

"Well, do you remember me mentioning my uncle Merk the other day?"

"The one who's like you, but who you don't know very well?" I don't manage to keep the note of scepticism out of my voice.

"Yes, that one. You see, I actually do know him quite well. I didn't want to discuss him with you before, as I wasn't sure if I could trust you."

"What gave you the idea you couldn't trust me?"

"When you mentioned your mum was Evigborn. But it turns out that my uncle and your mother were actually partners. Merk was over from Evig a short while ago, and so I was able to confirm it with him."

I'm stunned. I can feel my stomach drop to my feet, and no amount of wiggling my toes will get it back up.

"They worked together, but what does that have to do with anything?" I feel like Kriger is about to reveal the truth about my mother's death, or at the very least, tell me something new about her. Both are things I desperately want to know.

Kriger pauses and sweeps a hand through his raven-black hair. Taking a deep breath, he continues, "They were working to stop a smuggling ring between our two worlds."

All sounds of the cafeteria recede into the background as I focus solely on what Kriger is saying.

"They had two other members of their team, one from Evig and one from here. Connor was the team member from Earth."

"Connor?" I squeak. "He certainly never mentioned knowing my mother."

"It's possible he hasn't made the connection between the two of you, but he knew who I was."

"That's a bit unlikely, as I look just like my mum. But what's significant about Connor being part of the team?"

"Well, around fifteen years ago, the people they were investigating got wind of their investigation and intervened. I believe that's how your mother died, and Merk thinks it's possible one member of his team betrayed them."

I'm floored. I don't even have a response. It's the most information I've had about the circumstances surrounding my mother's death, and it's only a fraction of the story.

Kriger takes in my shocked expression and continues, "For a long time, Merk couldn't believe it was a member of his team, and they were all working together to find out who had betrayed them. But with no leads, they all started suspecting each other. Merk and Connor are working together again, but the other member from Evig, I'm not sure about her name, couldn't take all the suspicion and joined another group."

"Wait, why are they working together again if they don't trust each other?" The thought that Connor could in some way be responsible for my mother's death makes me feel both sick and incredulous in equal measure.

"I'm honestly not sure, but I think they're both testing each other out. They need to know who's responsible for the leak. Merk can't tell me much, only that they're working together again, and he wants me to keep as close of an eye on Connor as possible."

"So, you're a spy?" I ask, not able to hide the disbelief from my voice.

"Not quite. I really am here to train as a guardian, and I'd like to work here when I qualify. Evig is fine, but the need to live inside for most of the year does get to you. The fact that I'm training with Connor is a well-orchestrated bonus, which Merk wants me to take full advantage of."

"So, you're a spy of convenience?"

"Ha, yeah, I guess."

"Why have you decided to tell me all this now?"

"Because I think you have a right to find out what happened to your mother."

I couldn't agree more. Kriger is giving me answers to questions I've had for as long as I can remember.

We chat for a little while longer. I tell him what I saw Connor doing at the barns, which actually made me suspicious of Connor and Merk. Kriger tries to reassure me this was likely one of their missions, but I'm not entirely convinced. If anything, everything he's told me has made me more wary of everyone. Although, Kriger's opening up to me has made me trust him a little more, and it's really nice to be able to talk to someone about what's been going on without having to hide anything. When our conversation turns to Fram, we both go quiet. The reality of what we could be dealing with has been made abundantly clear.

"So, what do you need me to do?" I ask. Am I now part of his spy team?

"Oh, absolutely nothing."

"Huh?"

"This is my concern. I thought you should know the truth about your mother, and I appreciate what you've told me about Connor, but it's best if you stay well clear of all this. I can't get distracted looking out for you; this is serious stuff. I'll let you know if I find anything I think you ought to know."

I can't believe it. What a jackass. He is not my superior; we're teammates. Maybe he could use someone to watch *his* back?

I don't get a chance to argue my case as his phone rings and he ups and walks away, leaving me staring after him. Well, fine.

I thought we were finally getting somewhere and progressing towards a functional, trusting friendship, but clearly not.

In the afternoon, I arrive at the training field to see that Connor's already there, along with Ashleigh, Kriger and Freya. Fram's absence is clearly being felt, judging by everyone's subdued expressions.

"Do we know any more about how Fram is doing?" I ask Connor.

He looks over at me, and for the first time I spy a slight vulnerability in his appearance.

"She's still conscious. The doctors are hopeful there's no brain damage, but she has a broken leg and a few cracked ribs," Connor says and abruptly turns away.

I steal a glance towards Kriger and notice him watching me with a raised eyebrow. There's clearly a relationship between Connor and Fram, so it seems really unlikely that Connor's in any way responsible for what happened to her. Hopefully he wasn't responsible for what happened to my mother either. So, what on earth is going on at the Academy? I remember I'm mad at Kriger and so give him a quelling look in response, which he ignores as he turns his attention back to Connor. Doing the same, I focus on getting prepared for our task.

I'm really looking forward to this, as it's the best thing to stop my mind from going around in dizzying circles. Freya has already set up her equipment and is rapidly wiring me up. I've got a small camera, clipped onto my top, and a highly discreet earpiece. The reassuring weight of the blunted training knives strapped to my wrist makes me feel ready, although for what exactly, I'm not sure.

After a quick sound check, we go over our plan. Since I'm faster than Kriger, it makes sense for me to try and get the flag first. I catch a glimpse of it through the window of the small shed, where Freya will be conducting her operations. She's got access to my bodycam as well as a drone to watch for Kriger and other threats. As far as we know, there aren't any other obstacles besides Kriger, but we can't be too presumptuous. Connor could have laid some traps, and other people from the Academy could be here to try and stop us. We don't know whether Ashleigh and Kriger have thought of this too. Hopefully, being watchful and somewhat paranoid will give us the edge we need. If Kriger manages to catch me with the flag, he's likely going to get it, as I haven't managed to beat him in hand-to-hand combat more than a couple of times.

I give the maps a final look-over before getting into position in the forest. We're both equal distances from the flag, but at different edges of the enclosure. Now that I'm under the protective canopy of the trees, I can't see the flag, and the drones will have to rely solely on their infrared cameras to track me. We don't know Kriger's starting position, and he doesn't know mine, so Freya and Ashleigh will do their best to find us first. If there are any other people here, it'll be hard to pinpoint our positions accurately. I hear a distant gunshot, hopefully a blank one, and we're off.

Dried leaves and twigs crack beneath my feet, each snap sending out a flare of sound to those nearby. I don't have time to tread carefully and be quiet; this is all about speed. I'm watchful for potential traps, perhaps a false floor, but if I have any chance of winning this then I need to push myself hard. Freya's voice enters through my earpiece, confoundingly close given how much space is around me.

"I think I have him. He's approaching south-west from your position. He's moving very fast, but you have the edge for now."

"Great, thanks," I puff out.

"I'm also detecting a few static heat signatures. It's possible they're people. They're not moving right now, and I can't detect any that you'll be intercepting."

"Understood." The flag is still about half a mile away. I keep catching glimpses of it through the branches above. It's, thankfully, a white flag, so it stands out against the darkening clouds.

Oh, please don't rain. Trying to shimmy up a pole is going to be tricky enough, let alone when it's wet. If my Tk was stronger I could probably get the flag undone whilst on the move and fly it towards me. It would be a massive advantage, but I'm guessing Connor would have come up with a different task if it was that easy.

My legs are starting to burn, and it feels good. Not only am I having to work hard to keep up this pace, but the uneven ground and the need to swiftly dodge rapidly approaching trees is a challenge I relish. A grin pulls at my mouth. I'm genuinely enjoying myself.

The sharp snap of a twig, and the tell-tale whistle of something moving rapidly towards me, has me ducking down into a crouched position. I hear something strike the tree above my head with a thud. I don't waste time investigating but get up and push harder. Whoever is there is unlikely to be able to keep up, so my best defence is speed.

"Indigo, are you okay? It looks like someone is moving in your direction, and I think Kriger will make it to the flag very soon."

"They tried to shoot me with something," I whisper as I try to maintain my pace. "No idea what, so I'm just going to stick to the plan."

Freya doesn't respond, but I hear the comforting sound of gentle static, letting me know she's still with me. A few seconds later, I burst through the edge of the forest into the clearing surrounding the flagpole. I glance around quickly but don't see anybody, so I make a direct sprint for the pole. I jump up, wrapping my legs around the pole and locking my ankles together. I make quick work of ascending. It's not until I reach the top and unhook the flag that I look down.

"Indigo," Freya says urgently, "he's with you now."

Kriger is waiting beneath me.

I pause, right hand gripping the flag as the rest of my body is firmly pressed up against the pole. I have no idea what to do. I could try and throw some knives, but they'd be easy to dodge from this distance. Maybe if I shimmy down I'll be able to jump from halfway, which might surprise him enough that I could make a break for it. It's as good as plan as any, so I adjust my grip to make my descent.

I glance at Kriger one more time and see him holding the pole with one hand. It's then that I realise the predicament I'm in. The pole is metal, and Kriger is in contact with it. He wouldn't do it, would he? I'm up quite high, not enough it'd kill me if I fell or jumped – I have excellent bone density to complement my strength – but I would get hurt.

A small electric spark travels from the tips of his fingers onto the pole.

I'm falling.

I brace for the impact with the ground, but instead strong arms envelop me and Kriger holds me to his warm, solid chest.

The after-effects of the shock are still coursing through my body and I'm unable to move. Kriger holds onto me for a beat or two longer than I'd have expected, but then lowers me gently to the ground, and extracts the flag from my cramped fingers. His eyes rove over my face, focussing briefly on my lips before settling on my eyes.

"I'm sorry, Indigo," he rasps. "You'll be okay in a minute."

I can't even nod in reply, so I just stare back dumbly. He squeezes my shoulder before making a hasty retreat back to his base.

Half a minute passes before I can get back up and move. I try to contact Freya, but clearly whatever Kriger did has interfered with our communications. Thankfully, she was able to give me the direction he came from earlier, so I have a rough idea where he's heading.

I hold my head in my hands for a second, waiting for the after-effects of the current to wear off. I can still feel the impression on my skin where Kriger held me. I really don't get him. One minute he's being an absolute jerk, the next he's all gentle and kind? This is so confusing. There's no time to think about this now, I need to get the flag.

I run after Kriger, and it's actually pretty easy to track where he's been, as the ground is slightly trodden, creating a makeshift path. The last lingering current of static finally leaves my body as I pump my legs and arms harder. I dodge a deep hole in the ground, which looks like it was originally covered over with branches and grass. Maybe Kriger fell in? Hopefully it will have bought me some time. I spot a man leaning against a tree ahead. I don't slow down but reach for the blunted throwing knives strapped to my arm.

"No need to shoot me, I've been mortally wounded," the guy shouts, holding up a little white flag of surrender.

I decide to leave him be, giving him a slightly manic grin as I run past. The thrill of the chase is a lot more fun than I anticipated. With nothing to lose, I go all out and do my best to catch up. If I can get close enough to throw one of my knives, Kriger will have to stand still for a minute – unless it's a mortal strike – which should allow me time to double back to my camp.

I charge out of the forest and see Kriger up ahead. He's roughly a couple hundred metres from his base camp, the trap and the man must have slowed him down. I throw one of my knives as I race towards him. He hears my approach and turns to look over his shoulder. This slight shift in position causes my knife to miss him by a mere centimetre. Kriger appears to realise that if he keeps running, I'll certainly be able to get him with a throwing knife, so he turns to face me. Out of the corner of my eye, I catch Connor stepping out of Kriger and Ashleigh's base camp to watch.

Without much hesitation, Kriger draws a short sword, and charges towards me. I take a deep breath and hold my ground. I can aim my knives more accurately without moving, and I might even be able to use my Tk. I manage to throw two knives before he's caught up to me. One he dodges, the other bounces off his sword. I've no idea how he did that.

I quickly draw two more knives and manage to dodge the first few swipes of his sword, then deflect a few more strikes. I try to get around to his back to grab the flag, and hopefully make a run for it, but he doesn't let me. Within a minute, he manages to knock one of my knives out of my hand, and before I can reach for a replacement, his sword catches me on the arm.

I've lost.

The strike immobilises me for a minute, plenty of time for Kriger to run back to his base and win. Which he does, but not before he gives me a sheepish and apologetic smile. I stare at his retreating back, frozen to the spot. Darn it, this sucks!

I start to make my way to his base and to Connor, who is now walking towards me, not in a jovial way, but in an 'I'm about to rip into you' sort of way. I brace myself, setting my shoulders straight, ready for the inevitable onslaught.

"What on earth do you think you're doing, Indigo!" he shouts, towering over me. "You could easily have deflected that attack if you'd even thought to use your Tk, or you could have used it to make one of your daggers hit their mark! You can't avoid using what you have at your disposal. If you can't demonstrate an even basic handling of it, then I'll have to fail you." His face turns red as he continues his rant.

I cast a glance towards Kriger and Ashleigh, who has also come out to watch the show. Kriger looks like he's about to intervene on my behalf, but there's no need. I can stand up for myself.

"Do any of your talents hurt so much that they incapacitate you? Meaning you'd only dare use them in a life-or-death situation? Does it hurt when you hear someone lie to you?" I say.

I detect a slight flicker in his eyes. I only notice it as the rest of his face is so unnaturally still.

"What if I stood here and continued to lie to you, would you feel it? Let's see, shall we?" I continue.

The calm I felt before, whilst he was having a go at me, is swiftly left behind. I'm starting to see red. I'm not just angry at him, I'm angry about this whole situation. Why should I even have this talent if it's going to hurt?

I start telling him one lie after the other, getting louder with each one, watching for any sign that this is hurting him. I'm not usually such a vindictive person, but I can't seem to help myself.

With each successive lie, Connor doesn't even blink, he just stares impassively back at me. But there is something different about him. I don't think I'd have noticed it if he was moving.

Every time I lie, his left index finger twitches. Huh.

CHAPTER 8

The day I've been waiting for, and slightly dreading if I'm honest, is finally here. We're off to Scotland, and I'll be taking my first-ever trip through the Rip. I'll finally set foot on my mother's home world and this joyful thought grips my chest. I'm hopeful this might make me feel a little closer to her, but I'm also apprehensive I won't feel any connection and that the piece of me I share with her is gone. However, what's really dominating my thoughts as I load my bag onto the coach is what Kriger and I will face during our training exercise. It's likely to last more than twenty-four hours and could well involve someone getting hurt. The small one we completed last week, which I'm still mad at myself and Connor for, was a walk in the park compared to what we'll encounter. Connor and I are back on speaking terms, but it was tense for a while. I'm actually amazed he didn't discipline me for my outburst. Perhaps he realised he had overstepped the mark as well?

"Wanna be coach buddies?"

Startled out of my thoughts, I look to my left to see Rebecca's grinning, expectant face.

"Sure, that'd be great," I reply.

We quickly board the coach, which is filling up fast, and grab a pair of seats near the back. Whilst getting settled and chatting to Rebecca, I spot Kriger making his way through the coach. He gives us a distracted look as he takes the pair of seats across from us, dumping his heavy backpack on the seat next to him to stop anyone from sitting there. A minute later, I spot Ashleigh making her way towards us as well. She clocks Kriger's bag and takes the seats in front of him. She does, however, make a show of stretching and bending from side to side, allowing her tight black top to ride up, revealing taut, pale skin.

Rebecca leans over towards me and whispers, "I think she's trying to toy with you, rather than him."

I look up at Ashleigh's face to see she's watching me. I think Rebecca might be right.

I try to subtly glance at Kriger, failing miserably of course, but he's got his nose firmly stuck in his book and appears oblivious to the show in front of him. Looking back over at Ashleigh, I see her raise an eyebrow as if in challenge, before she plonks herself down onto her seat.

I'm relieved she seems more interested in teasing me rather than Kriger, and that he doesn't seem at all tuned in to her presence. I wish I didn't think of Kriger this way, but I'm pretty certain it's only a physical attraction, and I'm confident it doesn't go both ways. I think I'm jealous of Ashleigh's carefree attitude more than anything. Maybe she didn't grow up worried about what people would do when they inevitably discovered her heritage. Her talents aren't so visible, so it might have been easier for her to disguise herself. Forcing myself not to dwell on it, I instead focus on what we've got ahead of us.

I turn to Rebecca and we get chatting about what we think travelling to Evig will be like. I think about including Kriger in this conversation, given he's from there and completed the crossing more than once, but he's now got his headphones in and his eyes shut. He might as well have painted a 'do not disturb' sign on his forehead. Rebecca and I eventually lull into companionable silence for the rest of the journey, and I spend most of my time reading a book Cassie lent me. It's a historical romance novel, not usually my thing, but this one does go into a lot of detail about the weapons that were used. It's surprisingly good.

We arrive in Edinburgh at 8:00 in the evening, after a gruelling nine-hour journey. Seriously, I'm so numb from sitting down I'm not sure the back half of me is still there. We're all quickly ushered off the coach.

I take a quick glance around me to see that we're on Princes Street. The castle is clearly visible over on my right, lit up majestically against the darkened sky, and before me is the grandest hotel I have ever seen. The Balmoral Hotel is surely not the place we'll be staying? However, we all seem to be heading straight up the stairs. We make our way through the revolving doors, past reception, through a rather grand tearoom, and then we go down a few winding corridors until we arrive in the most ornate conference room. I didn't know conference rooms came with chandeliers. If it wasn't for the fairly standard desks and chairs, I'd think we were in a wedding reception.

Connor works his way to the front of the room and calls for us to find a seat and settle down. Rebecca and I grab the nearest chairs, dumping our bulging bags at our feet, and wait for further instructions as everyone starts to quieten down.

"Welcome to Scotland, everyone." Connor says from the front. "We are all very fortunate to be sitting in one of the smartest hotels in Edinburgh, and I expect you all to behave appropriately. The Luenn Academy has a long-standing relationship with the Balmoral, and I would not like to see anyone here jeopardise that."

He directs his glare towards certain members of our group. Thankfully, for once, I'm not one of them.

"Now, for the sleeping arrangements," he continues. "The hotel has set up dorm-like rooms for up to four people. Each room has its own bathroom, I'm sure many of you will be pleased to hear. I have lists of who's with who up front, so come have a look and get the directions to your rooms. Please settle in quickly, and then we shall all meet back here in forty-five minutes."

There's a sudden surge of people heading to the front of the room. Rebecca and I hang back and wait for the initial rush to die down. There's plenty of time to find our rooms and freshen up before our next meeting. When we do eventually get a chance to read the lists, we're delighted to see we're bunking together. However, Ashleigh and Freya will be with us too. I certainly don't have a problem with Freya, but Ashleigh knows how to push my buttons. I'm going to try and be the bigger person and do my best to show her it doesn't bother me. That'll work, right?

Freya and Ashleigh have already picked their beds when Rebecca and I arrive, leaving us with the beds nearest the bathroom. Hopefully no one will want the toilet late at night. It doesn't matter, the beds seem super comfy and the bathroom looks like something out of a magazine or, you know, a fancy hotel. I take one of the quickest showers of my life, the coach smell was beginning to linger, slap on a dash of makeup and head downstairs with the others.

It's not long until everyone has filed in and we're all sitting patiently, waiting for Connor to begin. He's standing up front with an almost amiable expression on his face. It might have something to do with the fact that Fram's standing next to him. I'd heard she was out of hospital, and she appears to have made a quick recovery, although she has a brace around one leg. She wasn't on the coach with us, so I'm guessing she came up earlier, to set up. I'm not really surprised she wanted to make her own way up, given she doesn't know who tried to kill her. It's pretty impressive she's still willing to be around us at all, to be honest.

"Right, everyone," Connor begins, "it's time to go over the itinerary and let you know a little bit more about your tactical assignments."

Finally. He's been so cryptic about what to expect, besides the unexpected, that I've been imagining some really elaborate scenarios. It'll be great to put some of the more worrisome ones to bed.

"You already know your teams, and I expect you to stay in touch with each other over the next couple of days to make sure you're all prepared. In order to simulate more realistic scenarios, we won't tell you the exact time or day you'll be starting. We won't have any teams miss our trip through the Rip tomorrow, but you could be asked to begin as soon as we come back to the hotel, or up to two days afterwards. This means that, as a team, you need to stay in close proximity to each other. This is why many of you are bunking with members of your team."

Ah, this explains why Ashleigh and Freya are in our room, and why Rebecca's all-male teammates are two doors down. I didn't see what room Kriger is in, but I'm guessing he's at least on the same floor.

"Right, now onto our trip tomorrow. We will be leaving here at 7:00 a.m. sharp."

Cue the audible groans.

"That's enough, everyone," Connor chastises. "It's going to take a long time to get you through security alone, so we need to utilise as much of the day as possible. Get your documents in order tonight. Wear appropriate clothing, so security can easily apply ink to your arms and, above all, get some sleep."

He gives us a firm nod before walking out of the room, with Fram trailing behind him. The other tutors check to see if we have any questions, but then quickly make their exit as well.

"Okay then, are you two up for a little fun this eve?" Ashleigh asks from the seat behind.

"What kind of fun, Ash?" I reply, trying to ignore the pain from her pointy chin resting on my shoulder. "I'm already knackered and it's going to be another tiring day tomorrow."

"No need to be a spoilsport, Indie."

The emphasis she puts on the shortening of my name makes me think I shouldn't be shortening hers from now on.

"Just a couple of hours of chat with the guys in the other room and some pizza or something."

This I could actually get behind, mostly because it involves food, and a bit of downtime to distract us from what we're about to do would be good. Also, I hate being called a spoilsport. I glance at Rebecca, but we both seem to be of the same mind and nod our heads in unison.

"On one condition though," Rebecca adds. "Whatever gathering this is, it doesn't take place in our room. I want to know I can go and pass out in peace when I need to."

That is a good point, and Ashleigh concedes with an opulent bow.

"Great, I shall chat to the guys and tell them to get us some food."

We've been given picnic dinners in brown paper bags and,

after a quick glance inside, I can tell that it's definitely not going to be enough for me. Pizza would be much better.

Half an hour later, the four of us are ensconced in the guys' room. It turns out Rebecca's three teammates are bunking with Kriger, and they apparently had no problem getting hold of a lot of pizza. It took me a little while to engage in the conversation, as I did need to devote the first bit of time to eating.

"So, Indigo, what's it like being teamed up with our Kriger here?"

I look up to see one of Rebecca's teammates looking at me expectantly. I was so engrossed in eating my weight in pizza that I didn't hear what his name was when we were introduced.

"He's okay, I guess," I reply with a hint of nonchalance. I mean, what exactly is he expecting me to say? That I'm starting to have a thing for Kriger, or maybe that his regularly beating me at hand-to-hand combat causes me to momentarily think of committing murder?

"I think I see what you mean," he replies, smirking, then claps Kriger firmly on the back.

Kriger shoots him a death glare, and it throws me for a loop. What does that mean? What on earth has Kriger been saying about me?

Rebecca, bless her soul, seems to sense the palpable awkwardness of the situation and promptly swings the conversation around to our trip through the Rip tomorrow. I listen with half an ear whilst the rest of me tries to decode the earlier conversation, with zero luck. I do my best to shrug it off and focus on what everyone else is chatting about, but I'm becoming increasingly fatigued. After a few hours, I call it a night and head to bed. Rebecca and Freya do the same, even Ashleigh joins us a short while later. We're all knackered and tomorrow is going to be a very long day.

The sound of several alarms bleeping mercilessly wakes me up at the ungodly hour of 6:00 a.m. Rebecca leaps out of her bed, making a beeline for the bathroom to grab the first shower. Ashleigh and Freya don't even stir, so it's up to me to silence the alarms. I fumble about in the dark, only knocking over one table lamp, until I find them all. I consider rousing my other two roommates, but until there's a bathroom slot, there's really no point, and it allows me to be next in line.

In the end, the four of us manage to get ready in the nick of time, and the hotel has provided takeaway breakfasts so we can eat on the coach. I'm a tad disappointed. I'd secretly hoped for a proper all-you-can-eat breakfast buffet. But the bag does have a reassuring weight to it, so it might not be too bad. The first thing I do once we're all seated on the bus is dive straight into my bag, and to my delight discover a trove of unhealthy delicacies. There's even a black pudding roll! I take it all back: this is awesome.

The excited chatter recedes into a droning at the back of my mind as I focus on the view from my window, after finishing my breakfast, of course. We're on our way to the Rip, which was formed in a local school in the small fishing town of Dunbar, about thirty miles east of Edinburgh. Although now it's less of a town and more of a military complex. From the pictures I've seen, there is still a small section of town that retains some of its quaint charm, I'm guessing for the tourists, but the rest has been taken over by the guardians.

No one really knows how the Rip was created; the student

who carried out his fateful experiment at the school died as a result. Other worlds have explained it's usually due to some large explosion that literally rips a hole in space. Apparently, nuclear explosions pose a risk of creating more Rips, and it is a risk, as more Rips would require a lot of protection. Particularly from worlds that are bent on stealing resources from their neighbours.

As we approach Dunbar, we drive off the main road and I can smell the fresh saltiness of the sea air. Inhaling deeply, my last flicker of nerves melts away. I don't know what it is about the sea, but it always calms me.

The coach passes through several security checks before we finally come to a stop and are promptly ushered off. There's nothing left of where the school must have once stood. Instead, it's a very large space with lots of boxy concrete buildings. Over the years, people have tried to make it look more appealing, after the 1970s brutalist architects built their monstrosities. But, other than a splash of paint and sections of wooden cladding, it's still a bit of an eyesore. However, what's inside is anything but.

As soon as we enter through the large revolving doors into the main reception area, the reflective glare of the polished white tile grabs our attention, swiftly followed by the array of technology on display. Clearly there are some pieces of kit here that are not available on the open market.

Security is understandably tight, and we're promptly arranged in single file as we make our way through checkpoint after checkpoint. They analyse our passports for Earth and Rip travel, our fingertips and retinas are scanned, and we have to walk through full-body scanners to make sure we're not packing anything illegal. All of these checks eventually lead us through to a smaller room where we're handed a piece of card that details our destination through the Rip. This card is used to get our arm tattoos and will provide access to the Rip. Only one person can pass through at a time, so we all require individual ones.

Even though excitement is building amongst us, I can't help but feel a little bored. So far, this has been like passing through an airport without any shops, or, more importantly, snacks. We can't bring any food with us, as there are very strict rules about cross contamination, so most of our stuff is locked on our coach. They're at least allowing us regular bathroom breaks, but that's about it.

However, things start to get a little more interesting when it's time to be tattooed. These aren't tattoos in the traditional sense, they're more like permanent ink stamps. You're allowed to get the tattoos of the worlds you and your parents were born on. Given my mother was Evigborn, and I have documentation to prove this, I'm going to get Earth's and Evig's tattoos. Some of the trainees, like Kriger, already have a couple, given they've previously travelled through the Rip.

The purpose of these tattoos is to allow people to travel to these worlds without an invitation. Essentially, they act as visas. Since this is everyone's first trip with the Academy, we're also getting a trainee guardian tattoo. This authorises us to travel to any destination as long as we're accompanied by a fully qualified guardian. This tattoo is placed just below the crook of our elbows and is an image of a long bow – the arrow gets added once we qualify.

Evig and Earth's tattoos are really beautiful. Evig's is an accurate picture of their full moon, not too dissimilar to our own, whilst Earth's is a picture of the northern lights above a floating iceberg. Each of these fill a circle of approximately three centimetres in diameter, so every world's tattoo is the same size.

I believe Earth's council picked the northern lights, so it wasn't country specific. A lot of other worlds picked constellations specific to their world.

I love our tattoo and can't wait to have it stamped on me, even if the machine looks terrifying. An operator, who seems unwilling to chat, wipes my arm clean with some kind of tingly solution, before drying it with the softest cloth that has ever touched my skin. She then types a few things into a tiny keypad placed on the side of a large metal arm, before swinging it around so that the circular white disc at the end is pointing down towards the underside of my right forearm. Before I can even ask how this is going to work, she quickly pushes the disc onto my skin. I feel a warm, slightly stinging sensation before she whips it off and inspects her work. Earth's tattoo looks back up at me. It really is stunning.

She makes quick work of the other two tattoos, before manhandling me out of the chair – she's clearly on a schedule. I stumble slightly as I make my way through to the waiting room, staring at my right arm in awe. Here I manage to join Rebecca and the others, and we now have only a short while to wait before they start sending us through the Rip.

My anxiety starts to escalate and my body tenses up. I take some calming breaths to relax. I'm not entirely sure why I'm so nervous about crossing the Rip. No one has ever been hurt before, but nor has anyone been able to accurately describe the event either. Different people have different experiences. Some remember nothing of the crossing, whilst others say they felt like it took hours, which isn't technically possible as everyone takes the same amount of time to pass through. Those who can remember describe a sensation of floating in a void, which is the only thing their experiences seem to have in common. I know we're able to breathe through this 'void', but I really hope I'm not one of those who seem to hang there for hours.

We start queuing for the final checks before we'll take turns to pass through the Rip. From an outsider's perspective, each traveller takes approximately five minutes to make it through. This includes the time it takes to scan your pass and tattoo, whilst you listen to the guardian's instructions. The Rip bends the rules of space travel, and it appears to bend the rules for time travel too.

It's not long before it's my turn. I look behind me to give Rebecca a final 'yikes!' look. She grins slightly manically back, and then I'm walking through the frosted double doors to the room beyond.

The Rip is contained within an opaque glass dome, outside of which is a small scanning booth for tickets and tattoos, and a guardian who does the final checks.

"Welcome to the Rip. May I have your card please?" the guardian says.

I manage to avert my gaze from the Rip's glass dome to see the young guardian holding his hand out expectantly, a slightly bored and resigned expression on his face. I'm guessing everyone has a mixed look of wonder and fear when they're here. It must get a little wearing.

"Hi," I reply brightly, passing him my card to be scanned. "Do you always work this room, or do they rotate you to give you a bit of a scene change, I mean, a change of scene now and again?"

Way to go, Indie. I was going for happy and friendly, but I think I came off as slightly deranged. The guardian looks at me with mild surprise. I'm guessing not many people try to engage him in conversation.

"They rotate us regularly. Need to keep us all alert so we don't get complacent. Something you will all learn about soon, I guess."

He scans my card and takes a remote scanner to my arm, then types rapidly into his keyboard and hands the card back to me for my return journey.

"If you could come this way, Miss Walker, I'll talk you through the procedure so you can pass through safely."

I think this is the first time someone has called me Miss Walker, and I really don't feel like a Miss Walker yet. I follow the guardian around to stand in front of the dome and look at him expectantly, trying to project a look of calm when I'm feeling anything but.

"Right, it's very simple. All you need to do is walk through the doors when they open, wait for them to close and then climb through the Rip. You'll likely drift slightly for a few seconds before being able to climb out the other side to the doors beyond. You may need to wait inside the Rip a while, but don't be alarmed, that's perfectly normal. You may experience a sense of weightlessness, nausea, dizziness and fatigue. All of these things will stop as soon as you walk through to the other side. Try to stay calm and remember, even if you think you're in a void, you can still breathe."

This does not sound as reassuring as he seems to think it does.

"You ready?"

"Yep." I nod, not looking at him anymore. I'm purely focused on the dome before me.

A seam appears in the glass, slicing through its smooth exterior. The gap widens and reveals itself to be two sliding doors. Once they stop moving, I step inside. They close behind me with a gentle swoosh. There it is: the Rip. I've seen artists' drawings before, as no camera can detect it on film, but they really don't do it justice. It looks like a very ragged tear through space, similar to the effect of someone trying to slice through fabric with a dull knife. The edges appear solid, and the gap is plenty wide enough to fit through. Inside the Rip, all is dark, but the outer edges glow like the colours of a nebula: rich purples, greens and gold.

Not wanting to wait any longer, in case I falter, I take a determined step forward and into the Rip. My right arm grazes one of the edges and I sense an extreme coldness, but nothing else. At first, I feel a floor beneath my feet and, glancing back, I can see the domed room behind me, but then it gets sort of hazy and distant as I feel myself lifting off the floor. I'm floating, like actually floating. If I was braver, I might try and do a somersault, like you see astronauts do in space, but I really don't want to get any more disorientated than I already am.

Looking around, I see the void is no longer dark, and the air has taken on a golden shimmer. It's really beautiful, and quite calming. Definitely a good thing, as I can imagine this being quite a scary experience for most people.

I've been obsessed with space for as long as I can remember, and this feels like I'm finally there. The golden shimmer in the air transforms into the shapes of distant galaxies and nebulae. Logically, I know I'm not actually in space, as the perspective is all wrong, but I don't care. I'm still filled with a sense of wonder.

Almost too soon, I see a mirror image of the Rip I left behind appear before me. My feet gently touch the ground and, with a deep sense of trepidation, I take my first steps onto another world.

CHAPTER 9

Huh, it's the same. Or at least that's how it appears. But the more I look around, the more I begin to notice. The colour choices on the walls, for example, are slightly more vibrant than you would usually find back home. The cloth used to make the uniforms of the guardians has an almost silk-like quality. The people of Evig generally look the same as us, with a similar level of diversity. However, here in the northern hemisphere, the majority look like me, with dark hair and very pale skin.

Once I've passed through immigration, I walk into a gargantuan, glass-domed space. It's breathtakingly beautiful. It's filled with plants, trees and even wildlife. I spot a few unfamiliar, but beautifully colourful, birds and butterflies. The space is so big it doesn't feel like we, or they, are caged in. The view to the outside world is muted by the slightly tinted glass, and yet it still feels like it's filled with light. I've heard many stories about Evig's relationship with the outside world. Aliens, who were highly sensitive to natural light, invaded them many generations ago, and they stayed. With a lot of mixing in subsequent generations, large portions of the resultant population have retained the sensitivity, and most of them reside in the darker northern hemisphere. There are even those who are so sensitive to light that they cannot set foot outside without total protection, and so the designers, engineers and architects of this world have been very creative in constructing spaces that feel like the outdoors. This being one of them.

I spot Ashleigh and Kriger up ahead amongst a small group from the Academy. Many of these people I now know by name, although we haven't chatted much. The person who most intrigues me is a tall, slim boy called Mana. He clearly has Malam heritage, as his dark skin has a purple shimmer, which is an uncommon trait. Having done some research about Malam for astronomy class, I can't help but wonder how many talents he holds from that world. In particular, I want to know if one of his talents is telepathy. Mana notices me staring at him and rolls his eyes in response.

"No, I can't read your mind. It's Indigo, right?"

I nod.

"Just to stave off the barrage of questions I'm sure you and others have, I'm only able to communicate telepathically with strong telepaths, and the only thing I can get from the rest of you is your general intentions."

I furrow my brow at this.

He explains, "I mean, for example, I would know if you intended to hurt me or…"

He turns fully to face me, eyes straying to my mouth.

"Or even kiss me," he finishes, raising one eyebrow up in an apparent challenge.

I return the eyebrow, smirking, and reply, "Sorry to disappoint." The others in our group are watching intently. My eyes flicker up to Kriger to see him watching us with a definite scowl upon his face.

Before Mana or I can say anything further, Connor and Fram appear and start counting heads. Satisfied we've all made it across, Connor starts lecturing about what he expects from us during this trip, which is basically don't do anything, and certainly don't wander off. We're due to head back in five hours, so we've only got enough time to tour Evig's history museum and then take one bus ride around the local area before heading back.

Fram leads us all to a group of people who must be guardians, if their uniforms are to be believed. They're quickly introduced, but I manage to instantly forget all their names apart from one, Merk. He's a very handsome man, perhaps in his early forties, who looks like an older version of Kriger. There doesn't appear to be any animosity or distrust between Connor and Merk, as they greet each other like old friends. Merk pats Kriger on the shoulder, so their relationship is clearly not a secret.

I cast my eyes over the rest of the guardians. They're a fairly non-descript bunch, but one is staring at me intently. Or, at least, I think she is, but whenever I look her way, she quickly averts her gaze. She's not very subtle about it though, so I'm pretty convinced she's watching me for some reason. All I can fathom is, given I look so much like someone from Evig, that I might look like someone she knows here. Maybe she knew my mother? Given that she appears to be a similar age to Merk, or perhaps a little younger, they could have worked alongside one another.

She has long, blonde hair and blue eyes, and she's currently standing in what I can only describe as a power stance, with her feet spread wide apart and her hands resting on her hips. Someone is clearly trying to convey their authority. I decide to ignore her and concentrate on what Merk is saying to us.

"Welcome to Evig, everyone. I hope your journey through the Rip went smoothly, and that you all feel very welcome here. Today, we'll be splitting you up into four groups to tour the museum. We'll then meet up for lunch before heading outside to take the bus tour."

Merk divides us up and quickly ushers us off. I find myself in a group with my team and Rebecca's, as well as Mana and a couple of girls who I haven't gotten to know yet. Merk is leading us, along with Fram. I'm a little disappointed Connor isn't with us, as I'd have liked to overhear any conversations he had with Merk. But it will be good to chat to Fram about what happened, if she wants to, of course.

In fact, it isn't long before Fram approaches Kriger and I at the back of the group. Kriger and I keep finding ourselves beside each other. I can't seem to stop thinking about him, and, the more I do, the more I seem to drift his way. I really don't want him to pick up on any feelings I may or may not have, as I'm genuinely unsure about his thoughts, and, of course, Connor has basically forbidden us from having any sort of relationship.

As I begin to dive deeper into my own thought cave, I catch both Kriger and Fram staring at me. "Huh?" I ask. Kriger chuckles quietly and Fram gives me a slightly frustrated smile.

"I said," says Fram, "I wanted to thank you and Kriger for your help the other day. It must have given you both such a fright, and I really appreciate you both staying so calm and helping me to get an ambulance."

Fram stares at us both earnestly. It's a little unsettling.

"You're very welcome," I reply, "although I don't think we did very much. How are you doing now?"

"Still a little sore on one side." She gestures at her leg brace. "The doctors are pretty impressed that I didn't hurt myself further."

"Does anyone know what happened yet?" Kriger asks.

"No one appears to know anything. As you're already aware,

I am able to make certain predictions about things, but, really, I just know when something seems off. For example, if someone is about to hurt me, I get the sense that I need to find a weapon. Or if someone is trying to find me, I feel the need to stand on a chair, so I'm more visible. But, this time, I only felt the need to run a nanosecond before I was pushed. So I don't think they were planning on doing it." She shudders slightly. "All I can think of is that someone saw an opportunity and made the decision an instant before they acted."

"That makes sense, I guess," I say. "But who on earth would want to hurt you? Did they see anything on the security tapes?"

"Who on earth, indeed. It turns out I was standing in a blind spot for the security cameras, so do let me know if you hear anything, however ridiculous it might sound." She turns towards me. "I want you to be particularly careful, Indigo."

I look back at her and feel an instant foreboding. I notice Kriger tense up beside me.

"Why?" I ask.

"I don't know, but since we arrived here, I have this strong urge not to leave your side."

"I'm getting the same feeling," says Kriger. "I don't have any pre-cog talents, or at least I don't think I do, but something seems very off today, and I think it involves you."

He looks pointedly down at me, and I feel my stomach clench in response to those emerald-green eyes.

"What do you guys think could happen?" I ask, breaking contact with Kriger's stare.

"No idea," says Fram.

Kriger shrugs his shoulders.

"But my feelings are rarely off. So, don't go anywhere alone today and make sure you stay close to Kriger or I, if you can."

A warm sensation fills me at the thought of being instructed to remain close to Kriger, along with a sense of indignation. It's becoming clear that my presence in either world may not be wanted, and I hate that I might need to hide myself. I'm definitely someone who'd rather fight, so this goes against the grain for me.

With my two bodyguards standing either side of me, we make our way through the museum, occasionally tuning into whatever Merk's saying. To be honest, the stuff he's coming out with makes Evig sound like a saviour to many of the worlds it contacted. I'm getting serious one-sided history vibes from this tour. Evig has always been generous with their help and resources, but after listening to how much they've 'helped' others, I'm starting to think they've invested a lot of time and money into making sure they're the ones calling the shots. As the first world to contact other worlds, they have always led the Cross-World Council, and by the looks of the technology and general wealth on display, I'm thinking they've also benefitted the most from it too. Interesting.

The rest of the tour is painfully slow. Apparently, it doesn't matter what world I'm on, museums are just not for me. I want to be outside exploring the world itself, not listening to someone, however handsome, drone on about past triumphs.

Finally, it's time for lunch. Now, as much as I love food, and I'm seriously hungry right now, I'm a little concerned about what might be on the menu. However, I'm swiftly reassured. As we approach the canteen, all I can see is trolley after trolley carrying a vast array of mouthwatering dishes. I have never seen anything like this. There are many foods I'm familiar with from home, but there are also foods I have never seen nor smelt before.

Given how hungry I am, I'm not going to take too many new things in case they don't taste as good as they look. Instead, I grab one giant pizza box and a plate of this purple spaghetti thing. It smells divine, even if it does look a bit like a muppet threw up on a plate. The pizza is delicious – well, it's hard to mess up a pizza – and the purple stuff tasted nearly as good as it smelt. I think if I had it often, I'd probably like it more, it was just so different to what I was expecting. It was sweet with an almost almondy aftertaste.

If we had time, I'd try some more food. However, everyone is starting to pack up and get ready for the bus tour. I quickly find Rebecca, and the two of us, with my bodyguard Kriger following behind, make our way onto the seriously swanky bus.

The inside feels more like the first-class cabin on a large aircraft, with generously sized leather reclining seats and a whole world of entertainment accessed from the armrests. As the bus leaves the side of the building, we're smoothly swept along a highway at an impressive speed, and I notice the road is mostly filled with similar looking vehicles of varying sizes. None of them have any discernible driver, so I'm guessing they've gone fully autonomous here. Not knowing who – or what – is in control of all these vehicles, our bus included, does make me a tad unsettled. I don't like the feeling of not being in control; it makes me want to try and get my driving licence when we get back to our world.

Even through our tinted windows, the scenery is awe-inspiring. The mountains are tall and craggy, with a delicate touch of snow on top. The valleys are deep and lush with dusky purple flowers, a shade darker than the photos I've seen of heather in Scotland. The whole landscape seems like a cross between Scotland and Norway, but on a grander scale.

I manage to drag my attention away from the arresting scenery to listen to our guide through the speakers in our headrests. Apparently, Evig has a lot more land than our Earth, but large swathes of it are uninhabitable due to its marshy nature. Most of the land lies within the northern hemisphere, where many people live, but because a large portion of their population is sensitive to light, most tend to reside in enormous glass domed communities. It seems a shame to have all this rugged beauty on your doorstep and be unable to explore it, let alone build a comfortable home and live amongst it. I'm sure living in a large community has lots of benefits, but there must be many who crave the peace and independence that comes with living more remotely.

I glance over at Kriger and see a wistful expression on his face, which must be similar to my own. I wonder if this is the part of Evig that he and his family are from. My right leg starts to bounce up and down slightly, a clear sign that I want to be up and about, rather than cooped up in this bus. The sight of the scenery is torturous, so much clear open space where I could really let go and move. Kriger glances across and down at my bouncing leg, and smirks at me. He's beginning to understand me a little too well.

The tour ends a short while later, and I'm relieved to be getting off the bus, but it's driven straight into their underground garage, so we still can't step outside. I quickly realise that we're never actually going to set foot outside, in the open air, as we're already being ushered towards the Rip.

Passing through security shouldn't take quite as long this time, as we've already had our tattoos done. Unfortunately, this isn't true for me. There's a flag on my file, or at least that's what one of the guardians tells me at security, and I'll need to answer some questions before I'm allowed to leave. Connor and Fram try to argue with the guardians, once they realise what's happening, and Kriger tries to speak to Merk about it, but they aren't able to do anything.

The guardian, who I don't recognise, grabs my arm and leads me towards a small room behind a row of check-in desks. I'm not even allowed to have anyone come with me. Connor manages to whisper to me that they have no authority to detain me as I'm an Earth trainee guardian, they just have the right to question me. I wish I knew what it was all about, and how long it's going to take. Fram and Kriger's warnings about not being left alone play on my mind as I'm led away.

I'm brought into a windowless room and directed to sit on a lone metal chair, which is bolted to the floor. I sit looking at two male guardians, who are behind a beautifully carved wooden desk, totally at odds with the room's austere décor. I glance around to see if there's a two-way mirror here, but all I can see is a spotlight in the corner, which may double up as a security camera.

I don't recognise the two male guardians sitting opposite me, but I do recognise the female guardian who's entering the room and taking the seat directly in front of me. It's the same guardian I spotted earlier, the one who was staring at me. Her blue eyes look back now, unashamedly scrutinising me. Her gaze is making me uncomfortable but, never one to lose a staring contest, I glare right back. She holds my gaze for a few moments before glancing down at the disturbingly large file before her. I do my best to ignore it. I've heard about the police back home doing things like this to intimidate people. Instead, I look at the security badge hanging from her neck. Her name is Forra. There's no last name, but the symbol for a fully qualified guardian dominates most of the badge.

Forra riffles through the file before pausing to look at me.

"Can you state your name in full for us please?" she asks.

"Indigo Elna Walker."

At the mention of my middle name, I see Forra tense, but she quickly relaxes and writes my name on her tablet. The fact she's using a tablet rather than paper confirms my theory that the paper file is merely for show.

"And what's your connection to Evig? I see you have an Evig tattoo."

"My mother was from here." I really don't want to talk about my mother, especially with this woman. I don't trust her, and I suspect that any information I give her will only put me in more danger. On the other hand, the only way I'm going to get out of here is by telling the truth, so I'll try and tell her as little as possible.

"Your mother's name?"

"Elna, I don't know her last name."

"How can you not know your own mother's last name?" Forra scoffs.

I try not to show how much her attitude is affecting me. Taking a calming breath, I reply, "Because she died when I was very young, and she didn't marry my father." Forra raises an eyebrow at this, so I add, "I don't believe my father ever knew her full name. If he did, he never told me." It is pretty close to the truth. In fact, I do know her last name, but it wasn't the name she was born with, as she was adopted.

"Was she a guardian?"

"I believe so, yes. But, again, I don't know much more than that; she wouldn't tell my father anything. I'm guessing she wasn't allowed to."

"If I showed you a picture of her, would you recognise her?"

This question catches me off guard. A photo of my mother, one I possibly haven't seen before? I nod and wait for her to show me the picture.

She taps her stylus a few times on her tablet, before turning her tablet around to face me. The sight of my mother causes a sharp pain in my chest, and I feel a shot of adrenaline rush through me. I nod mutely, whilst staring intently at her photo. It's clearly one she had taken when she had just qualified because she looks young and hopeful in her dark blue uniform. I've always known I look like her, but this photo must have been taken before she was even twenty, and it's like looking at an older sister. Her dark hair is long and smooth, and her eyes, so like my own, stare back at me. She looks happy. In all the photos I have of her back home, she looks happy but tired. Either it was due to having me whilst working a stressful job, or something else was worrying her.

Forra turns the tablet back towards her then reaches under the table to grab a jug of water and a cup. "We have a lot of questions to ask you, before we can let you head back home. It's not something you need to be too concerned about; we just want to verify your identity and your heritage. This could take a while, so do help yourself to some water and we can get started."

The way she worded it makes it seem like I *have to* drink the water. Things didn't feel right before, but now I'm really worried. Is she trying to poison me? Or am I being super paranoid because of what Fram and Kriger felt?

I don't get much time to think about it before the door to the room suddenly bursts open. Connor, and two guardians I don't recognise, barge through to stand in front of me, facing Forra and her associates. One is a giant of a man.

"Forra," the giant guardian says, "you have not been authorised to conduct this interview, and as these guests will understandably not leave without her, we have an increasing backlog of travellers waiting."

"Sir, we have a right to question people who pass into our world."

"That may be, but as she's part of a trainee guardian group, you have to interview her supervisors first, and you have to have my approval as well."

Forra starts to say something but he ignores her.

The man continues, "I see no reason why she's been flagged up in the first place, so I'm ending this interview now."

He then turns and extends his hand towards me to help me out of the chair, grasping my hand firmly.

"On behalf of the guardians of Evig, I apologise for the confusion. Please now make your way safely home to Earth with your fellow trainees."

I nod my head in thanks as Connor wraps his arm around my shoulders and practically pushes me out of the room.

We promptly reach the others; everyone has passed through security and is ready to go through the Rip. Apparently, there was a consensus they would all stay here until I could travel too. I know I wasn't in there long, but I am a little touched.

A few hefty back slaps later and I'm returning through the Rip. This time around, it feels completely different. Once I'm through Evig's side, I start to spin and get the sense I'm being wrapped in an invisible cocoon. You'd think it'd be frightening, or at the very least disconcerting, but it's not. The whole experience is comforting and welcoming, as if I'm burying myself in my duvet back home. It's over far too quickly, and before I even realise I've stopped spinning, I'm stepping back through Earth's side of the Rip.

In the evening, during dinner back at the hotel, the buzz of chatter is positively palpable. Everyone's experiences of the Rip and the bus trip on Evig dominate the conversation. I thought we'd be planning, or at least discussing, tomorrow's tactical assignments. However, I can't think about that either right now. From what I've heard so far, none of us had the same experience of the Rip. Some people really did feel like they were in there for hours, whilst Rebecca doesn't have any memory of it at all. I don't get to hear Kriger's experience, as he got swept up by some of the guys whilst grabbing his food, but hopefully we'll find a moment to chat later.

We don't get long to eat before Connor, Fram and a few other guardians walk briskly into the room. I hadn't noticed their absence until now. Connor quickly jumps up onto one of the tables, and everyone falls silent. They can't seriously expect us to start the tactical assignments now? We've only been back half an hour.

"No hanging around people," Connor begins, "grab your things and your teammates, your tactical assignments start now."

Yup, of course they do.

CHAPTER 10

It only takes Ashleigh, Freya, Kriger and I three minutes to get organised and meet Fram for a briefing. She tells us we are to track and apprehend a suspect who has travelled from Evig on falsified documents and has not returned in the allotted time. They show us a picture of her, and her last known location, Edinburgh Waverley train station, which is very close to the hotel. In reality, I recognise the woman as one of the second-year students. I had no idea they were up here as well. I don't know anything about her, and we – of course – are not supposed to know what any of her special skills are, but at least I'll be able to spot her in a crowd as she is a very tall, statuesque woman, with flame red hair.

Kriger and I quickly devise a plan, whilst Ashleigh and Freya set themselves up in a communications room ready to help us. They have access to live CCTV, one of the perks of being a guardian, and will guide Kriger and I through this.

Kriger goes and organises a vehicle for us to use, whilst I run to the station and down the steps towards the concourse to see if I can spot her. It's possible she hasn't left yet. I don't see her anywhere in the main station concourse, and she could be beyond the ticket barriers. As I can't access those quickly, I decide to investigate the areas that aren't closely monitored by CCTV, like the toilets, for example.

I run into the women's toilets, quickly flashing my Academy ID card at the disgruntled ladies waiting in the queue, hoping they don't look at it too closely – it states that I'm a trainee guardian. I jump up on the block of sinks to check out the hair colours of the women in the cubicles, but don't spot her. She might be wearing a disguise, but I don't have time to wait for everyone to leave their cubicles, and I would definitely receive complaints from the public if I barged in on anyone. They're not our biggest fans at the best of times. Instead, I run back out and check the few shops in the station.

I hear Kriger tell me he has a car waiting at the taxi rank outside the station. The sound of his voice coming directly into my ear is oddly intimate. I want to revel in this feeling, but I don't have time. We're on the clock here.

"Found her," comes Ashleigh's assured voice. "She boarded a train for Glasgow three minutes ago; you just missed her."

"Darn it!" I reply. "Car or train, Ash?"

"Definitely car, the next train isn't for another fifteen minutes, and there aren't any traffic jams on the M8 right now."

"I've got the fastest route mapped out for you," interrupts Freya. "Join Kriger and I'll direct you both."

I run towards the taxi rank, spotting Kriger instantly in the only silver car amongst a river of black cabs. I swiftly dive into the passenger seat and Kriger takes us up the ramp to the main road beyond at speed. I quickly scan the dashboard for the siren button and eventually find it above my head. I switch it on; the deafening sound is only slightly muted by our tin can of a car. Clearly, they're not allowing us anything with any real speed.

I really do need to sort out my licence. All trainee guardians must take an advanced driving course, which Kriger's already done, but I haven't organised one for myself yet.

I hold onto my door and seat tightly as Kriger takes a number of sharp turns. I hear Freya's calm voice in my ear as she directs us. My job right now is to watch out for hazards, and there are a lot of those.

"Cyclist crossing up ahead," I calmly say whilst trying to relax my death grip on the door. "Red car on the roundabout isn't stopping for us."

"Spotted," Kriger replies, without moving his eyes from the road.

We continue like this for the next ten minutes, until we're on the M8. It's quite late in the evening, and there isn't too much traffic until we hit Glasgow. Thankfully, most people hear us coming and move out of our way, so it's not long before we're heading down the ramp towards Queen Street station. Kriger manages to find a loading bay on George Square, and we both jump out of the car and run into the station.

"Her train got in two minutes ago. It was really busy, and we haven't been able to spot her yet," Freya murmurs into our ears. "We'll keep looking, but you've got a good chance of finding her in the station."

"Indigo, sweep out the left-hand side of the station and I'll do the right," Kriger says.

"Yes, sir," I reply, and he gives me a cheeky smirk in response before diving into the crowd of commuters. I hastily do the same and am immediately thankful for my tall frame, as it allows me to scan the heads around me. No one stands out, so I once again start checking the shops and toilets.

"Found her," Ashleigh says in my ear. "She's walking up Buchanan Street, heading for the shopping centre. If you're quick, you might be able to apprehend her before she's lost amongst the crowds of shoppers. She's now wearing a black baseball cap, and an ankle-length blue anorak."

I race out of the station and start jogging up the street, on the lookout. Kriger quickly appears at my side, and I'm instantly reassured by his presence. I'm not entirely sure how to apprehend someone in public when we don't know anything about her skill set.

Kriger grabs my arm and points up ahead, and I spot her at the same time as she spots us. She's standing near the top of the stairs, at the entrance to Buchanan Galleries. She's lit up by the lights of the shops behind her and holding onto the metal handrail, the same one Kriger is holding onto from the bottom.

The world falls still. We stare at her and she stares back at us. I could run and grab her, but I don't know how she'd respond. If any harm comes to the public, it's an automatic fail, and perhaps an expulsion from the Academy. Kriger could shock her, but I can sense his hesitancy to do so. If someone else touches the handrail at the same time, perhaps someone with a dodgy heart, it could all be over.

We stand there waiting for her to make a move.

She disappears. I mean, literally disappears.

Kriger and I both run to the top of the stairs, waving our arms around trying to find her, but she's gone.

"No freaking way!" I hear Ashleigh scream into my headset.

"Freya, Ash, find her," Kriger replies, all business in his tone of voice. "She surely can't hold that form for long."

"Kriger and I will split up and do a ground search. My guess is she's gone into the shopping centre, or she's maybe headed straight back to the train station. Unless she has access to a car?" I look up at Kriger, who shrugs in response, and I see a flicker of panic in his eyes. She can't have gone far yet, but with invisibility being one of her skills, this is going to be seriously tough. I really hope she doesn't have any more surprises for us.

"Okay, we're on it," Freya says.

Her tone is stern and focused. I don't think much ever phases her.

"Right, I'll take the shopping centre, as she may have dived into a lady's changing room. You take the station and George Square, in case she goes for a cab," I say.

Kriger runs off down the delicately lit streets without a backward glance, and I head into the shopping centre. The smell of cookies wafts over from the stall by the entrance, the cacophony of sound from the shoppers masking any tell-tale sound of running feet. This place is massive. It's made up of bending corridors and several stories, which means it's not wide enough to get a good view of everyone here. So, I decide to go for speed. I take care to dodge around people, which really slows me down, but I do my best to cover as much ground as possible.

"I've got her. She's getting into a cab on George Square. Indigo, get here now!" Kriger practically bellows in my ear.

I quickly spin on my heel and run back the way I came. I run as fast as I dare with so many people around me, and swiftly arrive at our car as Kriger is starting the engine. Once I'm in, Kriger drives in the same direction he saw her go.

"Shall I stick on the siren?" I ask.

"Maybe not yet, as I don't want us to go too far in one direction. She was heading this way a minute ago, but we need Ashleigh and Freya to direct us now."

"Good point." We drive, almost lazily, through the streets of Glasgow, keeping our eyes peeled and waiting for Ashleigh and Freya to point us in the right direction. Thankfully, Kriger managed to get a number plate, otherwise the sea of cabs before us would be even more depressing. We only have to wait a few minutes before Ashleigh's excited voice breaks through the quiet of the car.

"I have her! Wait, she's getting out. Oh, for goodness' sake, she's gone into another train station. It's Glasgow Central. Sorry, guys, you moved in the wrong direction."

"How far is it?" I ask.

"Not really far at all from your current position," Freya replies. "But by the time you get there, she'll likely have boarded a train and then we're back where we started. I suggest you hop back onto the M8 and we'll see which way she's heading."

Kriger and I do just that. Now we're waiting for follow-up instructions, I'm very aware of Kriger's presence beside me. Out of the corner of my eye, I see him intermittently squeeze the steering wheel and my mind goes back to the time when he caught me after I fell from the flagpole. He was so gentle, and the moment was so intimate, it really felt like something had shifted between us. I've no idea whether he thinks of me as anything more than a training partner, but I can't deny the pull I feel towards him anymore. Connor's words from the beginning of the year enter my mind, about not wanting us to enter into any kind of relationship. But was this an Academy rule or a Connor rule?

"Okay," Ashleigh says, her voice butting into my thoughts. "She's gotten on a train that terminates in Helensburgh."

"It's very close to the Faslane naval base, where the nuclear submarines are," Freya interrupts. "She may not just be on the run, she may have her own mission. We'll keep an eye on each station as she makes her way along the train line, so we'll let you know if you need to divert."

I programme Helensburgh into my personal tablet's map application, as I don't want Ashleigh and Freya to waste time directing us. It looks fairly straightforward. "I think we should swing by the station first, on the off chance we see her making her way to Faslane," I suggest to Kriger.

"Sounds like a plan to me."

Kriger follows my directions through some rather complicated road junctions, until it's pretty much straight on to Helensburgh. As we exit the outskirts of Glasgow, I can't help but notice the scenery. I've never been to the west coast of Scotland before, and it's really beautiful. Well, at least I think it is. It's completely dark now, but the moon is out and lighting up the mountains ahead. Not as dramatic as it was on Evig, but still impressive. I manage a quick glance at the calm waters of Loch Lomond before Kriger whisks us away. If we have to spend the night and manage to apprehend our individual here, I'm definitely going to suggest we take a few detours on the way back to Edinburgh tomorrow.

We drive down the long, steep Sinclair Street in Helensburgh, keeping our eyes peeled for our runaway. There are two train stations on this road, so she may be walking up from the one at the bottom of the street. According to Ashleigh, her train pulled in only moments ago, and they watched her get out and leave the station. Unfortunately, there aren't as many security cameras around here for them to utilise. So, instead, Kriger and I pull over onto a quiet residential street, where I release one of the drones we have in the car, which Ashleigh and Freya can control.

Now they have eyes in the sky, although they can only really look for heat signatures after dark, we can concentrate on getting to Faslane. We need to find a place to hide and either wait for our suspect to arrive, or for Ashleigh and Freya to tell us where to go.

The immense size and character of Faslane naval base is very hard to ignore. Set amongst picturesque hills and the Gare Loch, the concrete buildings and seemingly endless rows of chain-linked fence and barbed wire sit in harsh contrast to the surroundings. I look at the map and spot a smaller road up on the right that we might be able to use for cover. Who knows how long we may need to wait here. The road is narrow and wends underneath a small railway track. Leaves litter the road ahead, the recent rain shower having created numerous puddles for the car to pass noisily through. I really hope she isn't very close by, as she'll definitely hear us coming.

Kriger pulls into a small lay-by with a good amount of tree cover, giving us somewhere to hide and camp-out for the night. He turns off the engine and looks over at me.

"So, what's the plan?" he asks.

"I guess we need to scope out this area and find a good vantage point of Faslane? There may even be some abandoned properties or old farm buildings around here that she might use as a base."

"Good plan. Shall we split up then? I'll find a good vantage point and you check out what's here?"

I nod in agreement and reach for my go bag behind my seat. It's got my binoculars, spare blunted knives and basic tool kit inside, and I slide my tablet into the front pocket. It also has my night vision goggles, and I slip them on because I really don't want people to see my torch bobbing up and down. I see Kriger doing the same, before he reaches across and holds my right arm in a firm grip.

"Don't do anything if you see her, unless she spots you. Let's be sensible about this. I really don't want to have to drive across the country again."

"Agreed."

Kriger's thumb caresses the inside of my arm a couple of times before he releases me. From his neutral expression, I'm not even sure he was aware he was doing it.

We go our separate ways and plan to meet back at the car in an hour, unless we radio otherwise. I hear the very distant hum of the drone and look up to see its tell-tale lights blinking from very high up in the sky.

"Hey, Indie," says Ashleigh's voice in my headset.

"Hey, Ashleigh, would you mind scoping somewhere else out for a bit? I'm going to head up that hill, and even though you're really high up, I can still hear you. Don't want to spook her just yet."

"On it, Boss."

I roll my eyes and head up the road.

Instead of walking on the road itself, I move over to the side and walk between the trees, following the road's trajectory. It doesn't take long before the tree line is visible. I look around to see if there's anything I can use as cover and spot an old pillbox up ahead.

I wait within the trees for fifteen minutes, watching to see if anyone is here or trying to hide. Sensing that I'm alone, I break cover and head for the pillbox. I'm hoping to dash inside and use the small windows cut into it as a makeshift lookout. However, when I reach it, that idea is quickly quashed. The small concrete box has a locked gate, with a huge padlock in front of it, and a locked wooden door behind. Odd. Very odd. There are loads of these pillboxes back home, leftover from the war. Cassie and I used to regularly play in them when we were kids. I've never found a locked one before.

I flatten myself against the walls to better hide, making my way around the back to look through one of the little windows. They're all completely blocked from the inside, except for one, where a wooden plank has slipped slightly. Well, I can't actually see what's inside as the gap is too small, but I do have a very tiny camera that can stream live to my tablet.

I rummage around in my pack until I find it and set it to night-mode, whilst glancing furtively around me. This would be the perfect time for someone to ambush me because I'm out in the open and becoming increasingly distracted. I consider contacting Kriger or the girls for some backup, but it would take too long, and I want to get this done before we regroup. Sliding the camera through on its narrow holder, I get a good look inside.

Row upon row of small metal cases, with very familiar-looking warning symbols on them, appear on my screen. These are the same symbols I spotted on the boxes Connor put in the barn at the training grounds weeks ago. Dread fills my stomach. What on earth could these things be and why are they here? If they're as hazardous as they seem, then why would they be stored so publicly? Only one answer springs to mind: they're not supposed to be here. Someone has hidden them before they need to use or shift them.

I glance at my watch and see it's nearly time for me to go and meet Kriger. This is not something I'm prepared to handle on my own.

"Umm, Indie? I saw what you found from your mini camera. What the hell?" Ashleigh's worried voice invades the silence of the night.

"I have no idea, Ashleigh."

"Could this be part of the assignment?"

"Whether it is or isn't, we need to report it." I really don't want Connor to be the one we report it to, but given all of this is being recorded and broadcast live, we certainly can't hide it from him. I don't get long to think about it as Connor's voice is suddenly in my ear.

"Indigo, rendezvous now with Kriger, and we'll discuss what's happened."

I feel a mixture of relief and apprehension. I'm glad the decision about what I need to do has been taken out of my hands, but I'm worried about what Connor's response will be. I reach the car to find Kriger already sitting in the driver's seat.

"Find anything helpful?" he asks when I get in.

"Nothing helpful, but certainly something we need to discuss." I explain to Kriger about what I saw and show him the recording from inside the pillbox.

Connor interrupts, "Okay, you two, I've sent out a few operatives to investigate Indigo's discovery. As far as your mission is concerned, you need to act as if that wasn't present and continue to find your target."

I glance warily at Kriger. He returns my look, but then glances at the camera above my left ear, and I get the message. Connor is watching us, along with who knows who else, so we shouldn't give our personal views away right now. We're allowed to turn off our cameras and mics when we're resting, as we have trackers on our wrists that monitor our vitals and can vibrate to wake us if someone needs to talk to us.

"Understood," Kriger speaks into his mic.

"We're going to keep the drone active for a couple more hours. We'll let you know when the battery is low and needs a replacement. We haven't seen any sign of her, but we also haven't seen any evidence of her getting back on a train or into a cab, so we're pretty confident she's nearby."

Freya's voice is strong and commanding and helps me focus on what we're doing.

"That's great, Freya," I say. "Keep us posted. We'll set up a lookout and sort out a watch."

Kriger then fills me in on what he found, which is, essentially, a tree. Well, a sturdy tree would provide a good lookout point.

Kriger volunteers to be on first watch, and I realise how tired I am. Nodding in agreement, I settle into the car on the back seat and try to get some rest. We both decide, given our target's ability to become invisible, that a locked car is the safest way to camp. I've blocked out the windows, so no one will be able to see in if they're walking past, but I still feel unsettled and exposed. However, I'm so tired from the long and insane day that I manage to sleep.

What seems like only moments later, I hear my name being whispered and wake to find Kriger leaning over me, his hand gently shaking my shoulder whilst his thumb caresses my neck. It's a very familiar touch and, in my sleep-addled state, I stare mutely back at him, before my brain fully engages. Sitting up slightly, I reach to turn on my camera and mic, but Kriger grabs my hand to stop me.

"Not yet," he says. "I think we should have a quick chat about everything. I haven't seen any action and Freya has just taken over from Ashleigh on the second drone, so she'll let us know if there's any activity at the base."

"What time is it?" I ask, unhelpfully.

Kriger sighs. "It's 2:00 a.m., and here's some fruit and chocolate to get you going." He hands over two bananas and three Mars bars.

Am I that obvious? I happily munch through the food as I listen to Kriger.

"Am I right in thinking that the symbols on those boxes you found match those from the boxes in the barn back home?"

I nod.

"Gods. This does not feel good. I can't decide if Connor is up to something nefarious and duping my uncle, or whether my uncle is in on it too."

He looks so lost and vulnerable right now that I have a strong urge to reach out and hug him. But I don't. Instead, I pat him on the arm, but I feel even that reveals too much, so I pull back.

"I guess we just need to wait and see what Connor actually does. I mean, everyone has seen my footage, so he has to at least appear as though he's doing something. But we could always discuss it with your uncle or even Ivy later, and see what they think? I really don't know what else we can do."

"You're right," Kriger says, nodding. "Let's focus on the now, and address this later."

"Sound plan." I reach up and turn on my camera and mic. "Can you show me your hiding spot? Hopefully we'll catch her soon, then we can head back to Edinburgh and sleep in proper beds."

Kriger grunts in agreement and leads me to his tree. It's a big jump up to the lower branches, which is likely why he chose it, but it's not too much of a challenge. With our extra strength, we can jump pretty high. I leap and swing myself up and over the branches until I'm settled in a small yet comfortable nook. I'm actually a little proud of that display; it felt like I was some kind of professional gymnast.

I look down to see Kriger staring up at me. I can't read his expression from here, but he doesn't look away. I stare back until I hear his voice in my ear.

"Night, Indie," he says, then turns and heads back to the car.

I don't think he's ever called me Indie before, and in his accent, it sounds almost beautiful.

I stare at his retreating shadow before turning my attention to the job at hand: staying awake and watching for our target. It's very dark and late, an ideal time for someone to do something they're not supposed to.

To keep my mind sharp, I pull one of the knives out of my arm sheath and spin it over the fingers of my right hand. The action calms my nerves and helps keep my mind focused on the naval base at the bottom of the hill. I've got a good view of the fence from here, but I'm concerned we might be too focused on this one area. However, there is such a small gap between the treeline and the base that if we weren't right here, we could be too late.

"Hey, Indigo."

The sudden sound of Freya's voice almost makes me drop my knife in surprise.

"I've got a few new heat signatures near the treeline. One is making a rather determined descent down the hill. It's probably an animal, like I know Ashleigh and Kriger experienced, but there's something about this one."

"Okay, Freya, how far from me is it?"

"About one hundred yards north of you."

"Right, I'm going to get a closer look. Be ready to wake up Kriger if I get a positive ID."

I land on silent feet, very grateful to not have broken any twigs, which would disclose my position. My best hope of intercepting her is to take her by surprise. I really don't want to reveal that we're onto her, so I decide to head straight down to the road, keeping myself within the tree line. I should be able to see her if she breaks free and heads for the fence, or her heat signature if she's in invisible mode. With my increased speed, I know I can catch her in a couple of seconds.

I'm soon within touching distance of the road beyond and flatten myself against the nearest tree to wait. I can't hear anything except the blood pounding in my ears, and my night vision goggles aren't picking anything up either. I dare not speak to Freya or make the tiniest noise.

There.

The slightest movement, and then a very human-like shape slinks slowly through the trees. I press and hold the alert button on my wristband, hoping Freya can wake Kriger and send him over. Making my way through the forest, I move painfully slowly, as I don't want to spook her. I don't have to wait long before she breaks cover.

Darting across the road and throwing glances around her, she reaches the fence. She starts fumbling with her pack, and I see her pull something out that has a lot of wires attached to it.

Bomb.

I doubt it's real, but if she's successful in activating this thing, I'm sure it would be an automatic failure for my team.

"Kriger's getting into position," Ashleigh says, slightly breathless.

Clearly, she's just been woken up as well. I don't want to waste any time waiting for Kriger, as I have no idea how quickly this device can be set up. So, I decide to go for it.

I break cover and run towards her. She turns my way and spots me, raising her weapon – which I definitely hadn't seen – ready to fire.

CHAPTER 11

I come to an abrupt halt and see the look of satisfaction in her eyes. She's got me.

Kriger bursts from the trees like an avenging angel – I really need to stop reading fantasy novels – and the sudden sound and movement startles her enough that she turns to face the new threat. But before she can swing her weapon fully around towards him, I'm on her. I whip her right hand and weapon back, disarm her, and then lower her to the ground. I rattle off the formal arrest jargon and Kriger slaps on the handcuffs. It all happens so fast, it's almost anticlimactic.

"Congratulations, your task is complete," Connor says sleepily. "All three of you now need to make your way back to our hotel for a debrief."

Kriger takes the cuffs off our target, and we all share relieved smiles. I can't believe it's over. The tension I was holding onto gently slips off my shoulders, swiftly followed by exhaustion, which the adrenaline of the past day had kept at bay.

"You gave us quite the chase," Kriger remarks.

"You guys have no idea how close you were to finding me on that hill. I'm Shirly, by the way."

She reaches out to shake our hands and we introduce ourselves.

"Shall I drive everyone back?" she suggests. "I'm guessing

I've had the most sleep out of the three of us, and I'm quite wired right now."

We nod in happy agreement, trudging our way back to the car. Kriger and I settle into the back seat to rest; Shirly says she can use her tablet for directions. It's only a few minutes before we both fall asleep, I think my head might have fallen against his shoulder, but I'm too far gone to care.

We arrive back at the hotel a little after 5:00 a.m. and slowly make our way to the conference rooms for a debriefing. Connor, Fram and a couple of other mentors are there, but otherwise it's pretty quiet.

"Ah, there you three are. Head straight to bed, we can discuss everything in the morning. Ashleigh and Freya are already up there," says Fram.

I turn to face Connor. "What about the stuff I found in the pillbox?"

"It's already taken care of. A team have secured the area, and a full investigation is under way."

"Do I need to talk to anyone about how I found it?"

"No, your camera was on the whole time, and we have your video footage of the inside. It's most likely a prank. We don't believe anything really dangerous was being stored there."

I can't think of anything else to say, and Connor is just staring at me, clearly waiting for me to leave. Kriger grabs my arm and pulls me out of the room.

Shirly is waiting just outside for us.

"What did you find?" she asks.

I explain briefly, but don't go into detail, beyond mentioning the locked pillbox with boxes inside. I'm not sure if I'm allowed to speak to anyone about it. Hopefully I'll find out more at the debriefing in the morning. Sleep is all I want right now.

I'm woken in the morning by the sound of Ashleigh chatting and giggling on her phone. No idea who she's talking to, but I'm guessing it's someone she's into, given the look on her face. The blurry clock beside me says it's 10:00 a.m. Well, at least I've had some sleep. Freya comes out of the bathroom, so I quickly make my way in before Ashleigh can finish her phone call.

Once I'm showered and dressed, I feel almost normal, if still unsettled. It bothers me that I won't know what happened with the pillbox, especially given how similar its contents were to those hidden in the barn at the training ground. I suppose I could always talk to Ivy about it when we get back.

Feeling a little better now that I have some sort of a plan, I head down with Ashleigh and Freya to grab some breakfast before the kitchens close. We bump into Kriger on our way there, and it's only then I realise Rebecca hasn't come home yet, as Kriger's roommates aren't with him either. I really must be tired to have missed that.

"You heard anything about Rebecca and her team?" I ask him.

"Nope," Kriger replies, "if we're lucky, they might actually let us watch them on screen."

Unfortunately, we're not that lucky. Not lucky at all in my book, as we've missed breakfast, and Connor wants a very long debrief, both as a group and then individually. Shirly has apparently gone back to her hotel with the other year twos. We're not to know about their missions, as we'll likely have them next year. Instead, we're grilled for two hours about each decision we made, and whether there were alternative options we hadn't considered. I was pretty confident about our approach, but now I'm questioning everything. However, having not eaten anything in hours, I'm likely delirious.

When we're all seated together again, Kriger slips me a chocolate bar from his pocket as we wait for Connor to return and tell us our results.

"Where did you get this from?"

"You need to learn to never leave your house or room without supplies," Kriger whispers in my ear.

I turn my head to smile at him only to find his face mere inches from mine. We both freeze, neither of us taking a breath. I forget we're with the others and just stare up at those eyes framed by thick black lashes. He stares right back; his eyes drop to my mouth, and I think he's about to kiss me.

Ashleigh's indiscreet cough causes reality to come crashing back. We jerk away from each other, and I quickly divert all of my attention to demolishing the chocolate bar in front of me, cheeks flaming with embarrassment.

"Okay, you lot," Connor says as he strides into the room with Fram behind him. "Overall, we're pretty pleased with your performance. You appear to have done your best to keep the public safe, and you were still successful. So, in conclusion, you've passed. You can now have the rest of the day off, but be back in the hotel by 9:00 p.m. Dismissed."

As we leave the room, I see Rebecca and her team waiting outside. I don't get a chance to speak to her, as we're practically pushed down the corridor. They look exhausted but happy, so I'm guessing it went okay in the end.

"So, what are we going to do?" Ashleigh asks.

She's staring at me expectantly.

"Well," I reply, "I don't know about the rest of you, but I'd like to head back to Faslane, to explore it all in the light of day. Maybe just have a drive around and look at some nice scenery?"

"I'm in," Kriger quickly replies. "Would you, perhaps, want to check out that pillbox again?"

"Not at all," I primly reply, "I merely wish to see those beautiful hills in the daylight. They just happen to be near the base."

"Uh huh, sure."

"Well, I'm definitely up for some sleuthing," says Ashleigh, not very subtly. "What do you think, Freya?"

"Sounds like a fun day out to me. Count me in."

"But first I need to get some food," I grumble.

The others laugh and Ashleigh slings her arm over my shoulders.

"Come on then, babe, let's get you fed and then we can be on the road."

I think Ashleigh and I might actually become good friends; she appears to have backed off from winding me up and is now just a lot of fun.

In twenty minutes, we're back in a car. We managed to nab a non-emergency vehicle for purely touristy reasons, and I'm tucking into my second hamburger. Kriger is driving, yet again, as he's the only one with a licence, and I'm in charge of directions. This time, we're planning on approaching the pillbox from the top of the hill, so we're going to find a layby to park in before we covertly make our way down. We'll be able to get a view of what's going on before we get to the pillbox. I imagine we won't be able to get close as there'll be, at the very least, a cordon around it.

Traffic is, thankfully, light again today, so it doesn't take very long to get there. I don't want us to spend too much time here, as I would really like to do a little driving around before it gets dark. Kriger takes a right as we pass the welcome signs for Helensburgh, and we're immediately driving down a narrow road that slowly meanders its way down the hill towards the naval base. We find a secluded layby to pull into and step out of the car.

The air is crisp, and the sky is a brilliant blue, but I'm instantly tense and anxious. I'm sure we're not allowed to visit the pillbox, but no one has expressly forbidden it, so here we are. Ashleigh seems positively delighted to do some 'sleuthing', even Freya looks a little excited, but Kriger's expression is grim, which, I'm sure, mirrors my own.

I suggest that we split up. "Approaching the pillbox as a group is going to get us noticed, and there's little cover here, so we need to be careful. I would like to get one more look inside and see what Connor has actually done about this."

"Well, Ashleigh and I don't have the same skill set you two do, so I think we should stay together," says Freya, as she edges ever so slightly behind Ashleigh.

She clearly wants to do this, but perhaps doesn't want to be front and centre in the action.

"You're right, that sounds sensible. Why don't you guys head straight down the hill, then work your way back up the road where you can use the trees for cover. That way you won't need to travel long distances out in the open at normal speed."

"I appreciate you calling it 'normal speed' rather than slow," Ashleigh comments dryly.

I can tell she wants to roll her eyes at me.

"Okay then, sounds like we have a plan," Kriger chimes in. "You guys head off, and Indigo and I will split up and try to approach the pillbox from opposite sides. If we can get close to it."

"Yeah, I have no idea what Connor has done to it. He says they've checked it out and secured it, but does that include guards?" I ask.

"We have to be prepared. Ashleigh, Freya, do not engage with anyone. If you see someone nearby, send an alert to our wristbands, and we'll do the same."

Kriger looks at me, waiting for me to agree. As I'm so intently focused on him, I notice his eyes soften, or at least I think they do.

Gah! I have a problem. I nod my head sharply in agreement. It's time to go.

Kriger dashes off, and I figure he's aiming to approach from the north, so I decide to advance more slowly from the south. I could use my speed here, but I don't want to draw attention to myself. I'm hoping Kriger finds some cover soon, otherwise the game is up.

It doesn't take long until I'm nearly at the pillbox. I can't see Kriger anywhere, so I'm assuming he's waiting to see if there's anyone about. It's a smart move, but I'm not really in the mood for being overly cautious. If I do come across someone, I'm pretty sure I could at least outrun them, if they don't believe I'm a local out for a walk. If not, I can say I wanted reassurance that Connor's team were successful in finding the right pillbox. Not the best plan, but I'm too tired to care right now.

I haven't passed any walkers, not to mention any guardians. Everything looks the same as it did last night. The thought makes me even more uneasy because surely there would be some sign they'd been here. When I reach the pillbox, I see that the locked door looks exactly the same. Either they managed to open this and replace the padlock with an identical one, or they somehow had a key. Perhaps, most worryingly of all, they were never here. I reach the small window I used last night and shine my torch through it. I'd need my camera to see properly, but I can just about make out that the boxes are all still there. I don't think Connor has sent anyone.

I glance around to see if I can spot Kriger or the girls, but the hills are eerily silent.

Except for the sound of my wristband vibrating.

I feel the dread push down on me like a weighted blanket. I have no idea who has spotted someone, or where they are, I just know I need to make my way to the car. I'm exposed here, so my best option is speed. I take off in the same direction I came, trying to watch for obstacles and any sign of people. I don't see anything until it's too late.

A man steps out from behind a bush next to the road, and sweeps out his right leg, sending me crashing to the ground. I try to get up, so I can take off again, but he's on top of me, pinning my upper body. I'm still too far away from the car for anyone to hear or see me, so I need to take care of this guy myself.

"It's okay," I grunt, "I'm a trainee guardian." I'm hoping this guy is maybe one of Connor's watchmen.

"Keep your mouth shut, and I'll make this quick."

What the… what?

Not wanting to think too hard about what weapons he might have on him, or anything else he has planned, I use all my strength to buck him off. He lands with a surprised groan but is already reaching for me. I have two options: make a run for it, likely leading him to the car where defenceless Ashleigh and Freya may be waiting, or try to knock him out here.

I go for option two.

I wait for him to approach me and reveal what weapons or special skills he has. He looks Earthborn, but I'm not counting on it. It doesn't take long for it all to become clear, as he pulls a small handgun from his waistband and aims it at me.

Without thinking, I rush him. He doesn't even get a chance to curl his finger around the trigger before I knock the gun out of his hand and deliver a sharp blow to the side of his skull. He's immediately down on the ground, and out of it. I kick the gun into the long grass and race up to the car to tell the others and come up with a plan. Who knows if there's anyone else out here.

My heart is beating so fast that I'm having trouble catching my breath, but I don't have time to calm down because I'm not sure how long the guy will be unconscious for. I have to push through this.

I reach the car to find all three of my teammates waiting for me. Kriger's eyes widen in alarm when he sees my dishevelled appearance. He keeps calm and listens to me explain what happened, before manoeuvring me into the passenger seat with a cereal bar.

We decide to call Fram, as we feel she's the more trustworthy of the two, and let her decide our next course of action. Thankfully, she tells us to hightail it out of there. She'll send in a crew to check out what's been happening.

We do just that, but I don't feel the adrenaline leave my body until we've been driving for twenty minutes or so. Kriger keeps looking over at me, as if he's afraid I'm about to pass out or something. Apparently, Ashleigh and Freya thought they spotted someone approaching the pillbox from the direction of the forest, so they sent the alert to get everyone back to the car. Perhaps this expedition wasn't the smartest move of ours, but I'm glad we were able to raise the alarm with Fram. This is all just too strange.

We've still got a few hours to kill, and none of us wants to head straight back and deal with whatever's brewing in Edinburgh, so we decide to let Kriger drive us around the countryside. We're all trying to deal with, and in my case rapidly repress, what just happened. I can still feel the imprints of the man's hands on my upper arms. The musty smell of his breath and the sound of his deep, raspy voice have yet to recede to the back of my mind. I try to concentrate on the view through the window, but not even the deep green hills or mountains crowned with wisps of cloud can distract me.

We head over to Loch Lomond and drive alongside it; the water is relatively calm, dotted with small, tree-filled islands. We stop along the way for some ice cream – no matter the time of year I'm always up for ice cream – and stare out at the water. It looks so tempting, but the very cool air reminds me that jumping in right now would not be wise. I look up at the clouds gently resting against the peak of Ben Lomond, one of the taller mountains in the area, and wish we had time to climb it.

Kriger notices the direction of my wistful gaze

"Do you want to run up it?" he asks me.

"I'd love to but can't believe we'd have time. I don't think Ashleigh and Freya would appreciate us ditching them for a run either."

"Fine by me," Ashleigh chimes in.

I give her a surprised look, and she winks at me. She's up to something.

I look up the route on my tablet and see that we can only access it from the other side of the loch, and it would take us too long to drive around it. However, we get a stroke of luck when a local man overhears our dilemma and offers to take us across the loch in his boat. This stretch is fairly narrow and wouldn't take too long to cross. Ashleigh and Freya are up for a bit of a river cruise, and the man offers them, and a few other tourists, around an hour's tour for a very reasonable price. He seems genuine, and his wife is coming too, so I don't feel too bad about abandoning Freya and Ashleigh.

A short while later, Kriger and I are at the base of Ben Lomond. It's a fairly simple route up and doesn't involve any actual climbing, so we can run up it at quite a pace. In fact, it only takes us half an hour to reach the peak. We did pass a few surprised tourists along the way, and definitely heard a few grumbles and some casual otherworld prejudice, but otherwise it went pretty smoothly. It's a fabulous feeling running alongside someone who can keep pace with you, and that someone being Kriger does make it all the more thrilling. At the top, we both give ourselves a second to stretch before taking in the view.

It is breathtaking.

Thankfully, given the lateness of the year, there aren't many bugs to deal with, and the few clouds have finally lifted. We can see quite far, and the sun is making the loch below positively sparkle. If I had a romantic bone in my body, I'd be thinking lots of warm and poetic thoughts right now. But all I'm thinking of is the closeness of Kriger standing next to me, and the sound of his breath as it starts to come down to a normal rhythm. Out of the corner of my eye, I see him turn his head towards me, and my heart starts beating a little faster. I feel like he's going to say something, finally address this energy between us.

"Indigo, I haven't had a chance to properly check in with you about what happened earlier. Are you okay?"

It takes me a full moment to realise what he's talking about; I'd been so focused on the run and then on him.

"I'm fine. Well, better than before. The run has helped take my mind off it."

Kriger nods, as if that was his plan. Maybe it was.

"I'm pleased to hear that. I'm not sure what I would have done if anything had happened to you."

I look into his eyes and see how sincere he is. I really don't know how to take this; does this mean he has feelings for me, or was he merely unsure about how to handle the situation?

I don't get a chance to ask him though, as we're interrupted by a very loud group of tourists. I look back at Kriger to see the sincere, intense look of his has gone and been replaced by a mock exasperated one. He rolls his eyes and grins at me, before taking off like a shot down the hill. I laugh in response and chase after him. It only takes me a minute to catch up and pass him, and I hear his huff of frustration as I sail past. I can't run at full speed here as it's steep, and I really don't want to fall over and injure myself. Kriger, however, doesn't seem to be playing it safe anymore, as I can hear him catching up to me. He ends up keeping pace a step or two back until we reach the bottom. He then leans forward and grabs me, lifting me clear off the ground and tossing me behind him. I'm so shocked I don't even respond, but just stand there and gape, as he finishes the descent first. He turns around with a massive smug grin on his face, and all I can do is grin stupidly back at him. Our goofy smiles are only broken by the slow clapping of Ashleigh, who's standing a few feet away with Freya.

"Very cute, guys, but we need to get back on the boat and head off to Edinburgh."

The joy and lightness I had been feeling is immediately replaced by dread. I enjoyed our escape up the mountain and the respite it gave me. But now, the reality of what we face presses down on me. I have a strong urge to confront Connor about everything. I'm assuming Fram has passed the information onto him, but I hope she is, at the very least, keeping tabs on him. I look over at Kriger as we board the boat and see that he also looks like he's planning something. Hopefully we're thinking along the same lines; our drive back is likely the last time we can all talk privately about this.

"Freya, Ashleigh," Kriger asks once we're all seated inside our car, "do you have access to any tech we could maybe monitor Connor's calls with?"

"Why would you want to do that?" Freya asks.

I then proceed to tell her about all our suspicions, including those with the pillbox. "So, I'm guessing Kriger is suggesting that if we can monitor his calls, we might be able to see who he's working with or for."

Freya and Ashleigh look at each other, and then confer quietly for a few minutes. Meanwhile, I look over at Kriger. "I think Connor is going to question us, or at least he'll want to question me about the attack. It would be good to see what he does with that first-hand information."

"He might contact people electronically, of course," Ashleigh says, "and I don't have time to crack his tablet, or the equipment here to do it. However, I do have some small microphones I can connect to multiple earpieces, which look just like headphones."

I turn around in my seat to look at her. "And you just happen to have those with you?"

Ashleigh grins. "Never leave home without them."

"Please tell me you haven't used them on Indigo or me," Kriger groans.

"That would be telling now, wouldn't it?"

"Well, how do we get the microphone near him, and disguise it?" I ask.

"Oh, that's actually quite easy. They are super tiny and very adhesive, so all you'd need to do is subtly place it onto the back of one of his shoulders. I'd usually hug someone and attach it that way, but with Connor, you'd likely have to pretend to trip into him and attach it."

"Could we then maybe grab one each, and whoever he speaks to first is the one who needs to attach it?" I suggest.

"Absolutely, they're surprisingly cheap. Although, we should probably make sure we remove it from him when we're done. If he finds it later on, I don't think it would take him much time to realise it was us."

It's not long before we get to put Ashleigh's plan into action. As soon as we arrive back at the hotel, Connor strides towards us with a grim expression on his face.

"Does someone want to explain to me what the hell you four were thinking? Heading back to an area that was obviously potentially dangerous, and then deciding to do your own unauthorised investigating. It's no wonder one of you got hurt. I'm putting you all on a verbal warning. Any more bending or breaking the rules and you'll have Ivy to answer to."

He really does look furious, but is it out of concern for us or for himself?

"Indigo, you come with me. I want to hear exactly what happened during your attack. The rest of you, head over to

Fram in the conference room. She wants a word with you too."

The others turn and head to the back of the hotel, but not before Kriger gives me a pointed look, before tripping me up as I follow Connor. Thankfully, we were all prepared and palming our microphones, so I manage to grab Connor's shoulder to break my fall and plant the microphone.

"Sorry, I'm really tired," I mutter to him. At least that's not actually a lie.

Connor stares at me for a moment, before placing a hand on my back to guide me to a side room. I glance behind me and spot Kriger and the others slipping their small earphones into place. I feel a little better knowing they'll be able to listen in on our conversation.

Connor closes the door behind us and gestures for me to take a seat on the large sofa, which is squeezed up against the wall of this small, windowless office. He takes the seat at the opposite end and then just looks at me. Am I supposed to speak first? I decide to wait him out.

Sighing, Connor says, "Indigo, I'm not going to chastise you again for your foolhardy decisions. I want to hear what happened in your own words. Tell me everything."

There isn't anything about our day that I feel the need to keep secret, seeing as he knows about our investigation, so I give him a literal blow-by-blow account. He nods his head and lets me speak. I actually feel a little better for having told him about it. He seems genuinely concerned.

"Okay, Indigo. Thank you for sharing all that with me. I understand you think I haven't responded appropriately to your discovery, but you're just a trainee, and I cannot share knowledge with you about an ongoing investigation. You need to trust that I know what I'm doing."

He looks so earnest right now that all I can do is nod. I really do want to believe him.

"I haven't told you this before, because I didn't want to upset you, but I knew your mother."

I let out a small gasp. I mean, I, of course, knew this, but I'm surprised he's telling me. My note of shock seems to reassure him.

"She was an amazing guardian. We often worked together, and we were all devastated by her loss. I'm telling you this now, as I want you to know you can trust me. I would never do anything to betray your mother's legacy."

I'm not sure what to make of that, so I nod silently again. I guess time will tell.

I leave the room, with Connor still inside, and go in search of the girls and Kriger. I remember to pop the earpiece in right before I find them. They're sitting to the side of the conference room, apart from everyone else, and they look like they're playing some kind of card game. When I reach them, I hear the sound of a phone dialling and realise it's coming from my earpiece. The others all look at me, but then quickly turn their attention back to their game. It appears to be the slowest game of Snap I've ever seen.

"Hey, it's me," Connor says clearly through my earpiece.

I can't hear the other end of the conversation; the microphone must be too far away. From the strained looks on everyone's faces, I'm guessing they can't hear the other person either.

"I think we have a problem… some kids of mine found one of the unloading sites… I know, I know…"

Connor sounds really tired and tense. I'd almost feel sorry for him, but this is sounding more incriminating by the minute.

"That area should have been clear by now… uh huh… Well,

the thing is, one of my kids recorded it on their tablet and it's not just me who's seen everything. To make matters worse, those same kids went back to the site and one of them was attacked by an unknown assailant. I have to file a report later, which means Ivy is going to find out… I can't really fudge it, Merk,"

Kriger tenses beside me.

"I'll do my best to play it down, but if she finds out… Right, I'll do my best. Speak to you soon."

I can't hear anything other than the rustling of clothes, so I'm guessing he's hung up. We all look at each other, a mixture of shock and disappointment on our faces. I mean, I've always had my suspicions, but now they're confirmed, I have no idea what to do.

"Should we talk to Fram?" Freya asks quietly.

"No," I say, "those two are very close. If he's involved in something, we can't be sure she's not. We need to take this straight to Ivy."

CHAPTER 12

The bus ride back home is tense, to say the least. Thankfully, Ashleigh managed to swipe the microphone off Connor's shoulder before we boarded, so he should be none the wiser. She also has a recording of the conversation we overheard, or at least his side of it, so we have evidence to bring to Ivy. I hope Ivy can shed some light on what's been going on. Ideally, she'll take some action to stop whatever illegal activities have been happening under her nose.

Kriger sits down next to me, and I'm glad he does because I don't think I'm up for small talk with Rebecca right now. She sees me and gives me a not-so-subtle thumbs up. I'm relieved she's not offended, and roll my eyes at her. She grins and takes a seat with one of her teammates, who seems very happy to have her sit next to him. Interesting.

I glance down at my phone and see a bunch of missed calls and texts from Cassie. I feel terrible I've been so focused on my own drama that I've neglected her. I fire off a quick apologetic message, with many promises of long chats and chocolate when I get back, then pop my phone back in my bag,

I stare blindly into the distance, my mind replaying the events of the past two days. Kriger reaches across the armrest between us to give my hand a reassuring squeeze. I glance up at him to see my own worry reflected in his unbelievably green eyes. He holds my hand for a few beats before releasing it. I'm so tense and worried right now, and yet so hyper aware of Kriger sitting next to me. It is going to be a long ride home. Kriger manages to fall asleep not long after we leave Edinburgh. So, instead of wondering every thirty seconds about what he's thinking or feeling, I listen to some music and try to read, to distract myself, before exhaustion finally pulls me under.

We arrive back at the Academy at 9:00 p.m. and see Ivy's office window light is still on. I ask Fram whether we're allowed inside to use the bathroom, and, apparently, we actually have access twenty-four seven. I had no idea. Using the ruse of needing the bathroom, the four of us head inside and go straight up to Ivy's office. Time really is of the essence, and I want us to make our case before Connor reports to her on his version of events. Ivy's secretary is, understandably, absent at this hour, so we walk right up to her door and knock.

"Enter," she calls from inside.

We all push into her office, and I immediately feel like we're doing something very wrong. Telling on someone who's supposed to be our mentor is not something one can be unaffected by. I feel like we're betraying him, which, of course, we are, but only because he betrayed us first.

"I'm assuming you four have a good reason to be here at this hour?"

Ivy looks tired, her hair is dishevelled and there are noticeable bags under her eyes.

Kriger is the first to speak and explains what's been going on. We all chime in with what we've witnessed, and it takes us at least ten minutes to get through it all. During this time, Ivy is quiet but looks increasingly alert and angry, which is hardly surprising.

"Please pass over this evidence you have so I can see it for myself."

Ashleigh hands it over to her and helps her set it up so she can watch the video footage I took, along with the audio recording of Connor. We all stand there silently watching, waiting to see what her response is going to be. When she's finished listening to the recording, she sighs and looks at each of us in turn.

"Thank you for bringing this to my attention. It is, of course, a very serious matter, and I want you to rest assured we will get to the bottom of this. In the meantime, I'd like you all to go home and get some sleep. I will take it from here."

"What's going happen to Connor?" I ask.

"Mr Fischer will be properly investigated by the Luenn Academy and then the results of the investigation will be passed on to the relevant authorities. You are not in a position to know more, and I suggest you head straight home so you can recover from your ordeals. Good night."

Well, it's clear we're not wanted here. Feeling thoroughly dismissed, we head back out of the building and into the night.

"Everyone okay getting home by themselves?" I ask. Heads nod back at me; everyone looks incredibly tired. Without another word, we head off to our respective homes. My bike is still locked up outside the Academy, so I walk over and get set up to ride home. A hand on my shoulder startles me, and I turn around to find Kriger standing beside me with a concerned look on his face.

"You okay to cycle home by yourself?"

"Of course. Why, do you have a bad feeling or something?"

"Actually, yeah, I do. Or at least I think I do? I don't know." He sighs and rubs his hand over his face. "I feel this need to protect you, but I can't tell if it's because you're in some kind of danger or if I just want to be around you."

I'm taken aback by his very open admission. "I'm not really sure what to say to that." I'm really not, this doesn't seem like the time to confess all. I'm not even sure if he really admitted to having feelings for me. This is all so confusing.

"You don't need to say anything. Could you just send me a message when you get back, to let me know if you got home okay?" He looks almost embarrassed.

"Sure, I can do that. Night, Kriger."

"Night, Indie." He turns and heads home.

I do the same, although the ride home isn't easy. I can't shake the sensation that someone is watching me. I decide to take the longer route and stay on the main roads. If someone is trying to follow me, they're less likely to confront me out in the open. A short while later, I reach home and run inside and lock the doors. My dad is already up in his room, but he pokes his head out when he hears me come in.

"How was your trip?"

"It was great, actually." I cringe slightly at the blatant lie. "I got to see a little of Evig, and we passed our assessment." I'd like to tell him more about what happened on Evig, and during our assessment, but I really don't want to worry him or add fuel to the fire of our disagreement.

"I'm exhausted, so I'll head straight to bed."

"You need me to make you some food?"

I smile; he knows me so well. "That's okay, Dad, I'll make myself a quick something before I go to sleep."

"Okay, well, if you're sure. Have a good night."

I walk into the kitchen and wait until I hear the snick of his bedroom door before I pull out my tablet. I send Kriger a quick message, to let him know I got home safe. He replies with a smiley face and a thumbs up. Not very romantic, but then I'm not sure what we are right now. I'm too tired to think much more about it, so I make myself a sandwich then head to bed.

In the morning, I'm woken up by the sound of my phone ringing. It's Cassie. It's really good to hear her voice. We start chatting and I tell her what I can about our trip to Scotland, although I have to leave a lot out.

We've been chatting for about half an hour when I get a message from Kriger on my tablet, shortly followed by one from Ashleigh, both about the same thing. There's a warrant out for Connor's arrest and there's a bit of a standoff in the market square in the city centre. I apologise to Cassie, making yet more promises to have a longer catch up soon, as I want to head into town to see what's happening. I shout up to Dad that I'm heading to the Academy to do some training. He's busy on a work call so gives me a silent wave with the phone pressed firmly to his ear. I grab my bike and pedal as fast as I dare into town.

I arrive in the market square and see quite a crowd has gathered. It doesn't take long to spot Kriger, as he's a good head taller than most of the people here. When he spots me, an unreadable expression crosses his face. I'm not sure if it's relief or pleasure. I make my way over to him and am immediately pressed up against him as the crowd tries to surge forwards. Kriger grabs my hand, lacing his fingers with mine. I look up at him, and he gives my hand a squeeze before pulling me further into the crowd.

Connor's flat is up ahead, and we can see a lot of armed guardians surrounding the entrance. My stomach tightens at the thought that this arrest could go south, fast. Kriger seems to realise the same thing and edges us around and behind the operation at hand. I spot Ivy, standing beside one of the guardians with a large megaphone. She looks fierce in a black tailored trouser suit, with her hair pinned severely back. She may not be the easiest person to get along with, but I do admire her, and like to think I'll be a little like her someday.

"Mr Fischer, we will ask one more time: come out with your hands above your head," the guardian standing next to Ivy calls out.

I see a slight movement at one of the ground floor windows, then the front door opens. I have no idea why it's taken so long for Connor to come out, or why so many armed guards are needed. This feels more like a show than a legitimate arrest. I grip Kriger's hand tighter as Connor emerges from the building with his hands raised high above his head. His expression is grim but resigned, quite the opposite of Ivy's. She looks positively delighted now that he's made an appearance.

She raises her megaphone to speak. "Thank you for finally joining us, Mr Fischer." Ivy glances around at the crowd, clearly checking she has everyone's attention before continuing. "We are arresting you for smuggling otherworld weapons and narcotics, and for conspiring with otherworld governments to use our planet's people as test subjects for their controversial and unsanctioned experiments."

The crowd, including me, gasps audibly. I had an idea about the smuggling, but using Earthborns as unknowing test subjects? This is too incredible. She must have been making a case against him for months, if not years, to have this kind of evidence. I look over at Connor, to see his reaction, but his face is completely unreadable. He merely stares at Ivy, waiting for the inevitable.

Ivy continues, "We have mountains of evidence against you, and I know for a fact you're guilty, and the one who's been in charge of this ghastly business."

If I hadn't been so focused on Connor, I would have missed it, but his left index finger just twitched. Ivy's lying.

"You're lying!" I shout to Ivy.

I can't believe I just did that. Everyone turns towards me, in shock, including Kriger. I look at him. "Connor's finger twitches every time he hears a lie, and it just twitched when Ivy spoke," I whisper furiously.

Kriger doesn't respond. Instead, he pulls me slightly behind him, obscuring my view of Ivy. Unsurprisingly, no one is taking me seriously, but I've clearly rattled some people, as Connor is rapidly bundled into a car and driven off. Ivy gets into her car to drive away too, but not before giving me a quelling look over Kriger's shoulder. I think I've made myself an enemy.

"You shouldn't have shouted out, even if you're right," says Kriger.

He's turned around to look at me with a very worried expression on his face.

"You've put a target on your back, and I can't be around to protect you all the time."

"I don't need you to protect me, I can protect myself." I'm actually quite insulted he thinks I need his protection. I do, however, agree that I should not have shouted out.

"I didn't mean it like that," he sighs and looks up at the sky as if for inspiration.

The crowd has started to disperse, so we have a little more room, but he doesn't let go of my hand. Instead, he pulls me towards him, bringing his head down, and presses his lips against mine.

My nose is filled with the smell of his aftershave, and the feel of his lips is firm but gentle, sending a zap of electricity down my spine. If I didn't know better, I'd say he shocked me. It takes me a couple of seconds to get over my surprise, before I return to my senses and kiss him back. I lift my hands up to run my fingers through his feathery soft hair. I didn't realise kissing him would feel like this. The buzz of the outside world is a distant memory; all I can feel are his lips on mine and his hands around my waist. He pulls back all too soon.

"All I meant is that I worry about you because I like you. I don't know what I'd do if something happened to you."

"Kriger… I…" I'm actually lost for words. Whether that's from his declaration or his kiss, I'm not sure. I can still taste him on my lips. "I like you too." Wow, Indie, what a wordsmith you are. But it seems to be enough for Kriger, who squeezes my waist and gives me a small, private smile before his face becomes all business once again.

"We need to formulate a plan. If Connor is as innocent as you suspect, or if maybe he was working with Ivy and she turned on him, we need to get some help."

It takes me a moment to switch gears before I respond, "Agreed. Maybe we need to talk to Fram and Merk? I'm not sure who else we could contact at this point."

"Okay, I actually think Merk is on Earth at the moment, as we were supposed to meet this evening. I'll find a phone that can't be traced and give him a call. I don't see the point of taking unnecessary risks here."

"Good plan. I'll head to the Academy and see if I can find Fram, or at least find out where she lives. Meet you back at the Academy in an hour?"

"Meet you then."

He pulls me towards him and hugs me, before kissing me again, briefly, on the lips. He releases me after a final hug and then disappears into the crowd. I stare after him for a couple of beats, my fingers brushing my lips, before giving myself a mental slap and heading off towards the Academy.

The entrance to the Academy is buzzing with people and chatter. Clearly, news about Connor's arrest has spread fast, and I keep hearing his name mentioned alongside mine. I must have made more of a scene than I realised. I spy Jed and he catches my eye, gesturing with his head towards one of the alcoves behind him. I head over, hoping he'll give me some information about Fram.

"Hey, are you okay? I heard what happened."

"Thanks. Yeah, I'm fine. Do you know where Fram is? I really need to speak to her."

"Of course, of course. She should be in her office. I'll walk you there."

"Thanks, I really appreciate it."

We walk a short way towards the stairs, and I realise Jed is probably a great person to question as well, given how involved he's been with Ivy. "Did you know anything about the investigation into Connor? It all seems so sudden."

"I've heard rumours, you know, but I did hear about what happened with you in Scotland. So, I'm guessing that's what really got things moving."

I can't help but feel a little guilty. Should I have waited to go to Ivy? Is Connor actually innocent, or am I wasting my time? I am so in my own head that I don't pay attention to where we are, then find myself in a small room, alone with Jed. I turn to look at him, but all I see is a black hammer coming towards my head.

And then nothing.

A flash of light, an intense pain in my head, and the sense of being jostled about are all I am aware of before the blackness consumes me once more.

I wake up. Piercingly bright light shines through my closed lids, the intensity of it making my headache worse. I gingerly open my eyes and struggle into a sitting position; something is holding my arms back.

I'm on the roof of a very tall building, in a city I don't recognise, with the hot sun beating down on me. My arms are bound to a metal pipe behind me and my ankles are shackled together. Panic rises in my chest, and I look frantically around, trying to figure out what's happening.

"Welcome to Malam, Niece," a woman's voice calls out from behind me.

I look back and see a familiar face: the guardian from Evig, I think her name is Forra.

Wait, did she say 'Malam'?

Hang on, did she say 'niece'!

CHAPTER 13

"Niece? Did you call me your niece? Why am I here? We can't possibly be on Malam, I'd remember travelling across the Rip," I say, unable to keep the panic from my voice. I think I'm hyperventilating; I can't seem to take in enough air. This is clearly not a warm family welcome. Well, I am baking here under this intense sun, it's incredibly hot, but being tied to this metal pipe does not fill me with hope for our relationship.

"You heard me correctly," Forra replies, looking down at my huddled appearance with disdain.

"You may feel a little groggy from the drugs Jed gave you, after he knocked you unconscious, which is how I managed to keep you from waking when we smuggled you across the Rip."

"We? Is Jed here then?"

"Not Jed, I have other people to help me. Some you have grown quite close with, I hear."

My heart stops. Close with? An image of Kriger quickly flashes through my mind, but I shut it down. That's a question for later. I really need to get a grasp on what on earth is happening. I decide to get her talking, so I can give myself a minute to get it together.

"So, how are we related?"

"I'm your mother's sister. We didn't grow up together as our parents had her adopted before I was born; they were too young at the time."

There's a gleam of delight in her eyes as she tells me this.

"Sadly, she died before she could inherit our parents' fortune. Something I'd be willing to share with you if you'd like to join me in my business."

"Your business?" Why on earth are we talking about businesses? I have an increasingly strong suspicion she's responsible for my mother's death.

"My business. Your mother and the others in our group would never have wanted to help; they were all so law-abiding. I just bend the laws a little to deliver people things they need. No real harm in that." She shrugs.

Dawning realisation hits me hard. She was the one who was responsible for the smuggling, or at least some of it. She must have been the fourth member of the group, after Connor, Merk and my mother. I'm guessing she's got a lot of people under her thumb, particularly if this is how she usually runs 'business' meetings.

"Why else do you think we're on Malam?" she continues. "Money is everything here, particularly inside the city walls. They really don't care what you do, as long as you pay."

I think I'm going to be sick. The heat is really starting to get to me, not to mention that I'm at the mercy of the person who killed my mother. I mean, I can't be sure, but the evidence is really stacking up.

"Given we're family and all, I'd be happy for you to join and help me grow this business further."

Her eyes look at me expectantly, for what I'm not sure. I don't believe for a minute she wants my help because there are far better ways for her to go about getting it. Maybe she needs me to sign away my inheritance rights because of her parents' will, or to 'confess' something on camera? I have a strong feeling, however, that I'm not ever meant to leave the roof of this building.

I try to subtly manoeuvre my wrists and ankles in their cuffs. Perhaps they're not as tight as they feel, or maybe if I use my Tk, I could bend them enough and slip free? I start to attempt it, but Forra notices.

She raises an eyebrow, cocking her head to one side. "I guess that answers my question then. You're clearly only concerned for your wellbeing. Well, you're right to be worried. It's still very early in the morning, and you have no protection up here from the sun's rays, which are a lot stronger than yours back home. All that lovely, delicate skin will blister in no time at all."

There's a kind of manic delight in her expression; she's really enjoying this. She looks down at my ankles, where I was focussing my Tk.

"Ah, I see what you're doing there. I heard about your restricted Telekinesis."

Restricted?

"Your mother was wise to limit your true abilities. Very difficult talent to control, I hear." She looks closely at my face. "And I see the headache has already started. Good luck with that."

She's right. The pain has already made its presence known behind my right eye, causing me to squint up at her. But who told her about it? Jed, maybe? How does she know my mother limited it? Did my mum tell Forra when they were working together?

"Did Jed tell you about my Tk?"

"Actually, no, I believe it was your teammate who told me," she replies with a smug smile.

Cold fills my veins. Surely that can't be true. I really don't want to believe Kriger betrayed me. He's working with Merk, not Forra. But he was the only one who knew I'd gone back to the Academy, and he called me to town when Connor was being arrested.

I think I'm going to throw up. The heat and sense of betrayal is too much. Forra starts laughing at my clear distress, before crouching down in front of me, and getting right in my face.

"I would love to kill you right now," she whispers, "but sudden deaths send out a loud telepathic cry. Wouldn't want any strong telepaths nearby to pick up on that. Better to let you die slowly, and painfully, instead."

She reaches out to brush some damp hair off my face. I'm already sweating profusely.

"Your mother was lucky I was in a hurry; her death was quick and relatively painless. Elna thought we were good friends; she had no idea who I truly was. Not until the end, at least. I might have let her live longer if she hadn't discovered what I was up to." She smiles almost sweetly at me.

"But she was your sister," I say, almost to myself. I can't believe this horror of a person before me is my aunt. The thought of my mum dying by her hands, after learning she was her one and only blood relative, is too much.

"She was, but only in one sense." Forra's tone shifts to one of righteous anger. "I was our parents' true child. I'm the one they chose to raise."

She sighs, her anger seeming to disappear as quickly as it came, making her seem even more unhinged.

"Took me a while to find you though. Elna lied to me about your name, and your father's. It was the pain you experienced with your Tk that led me to find you. It's a rare thing. Your mother had to restrict yours, as it was causing her problems with her pregnancy. She used her own Tk to do it."

Forra stands and is now looming over me.

"I guess she was always a little suspicious of me, or at least of someone in our group, to want to keep her home life private."

Forra gives me a final once-over, before retreating towards the door to the internal stairs.

She stops, with one hand on the door. "Oh, and don't bother screaming for help. We're too high up here, and no one would bother to help you anyway, unless you paid them."

And with those final words, she walks through the open doorway, leaving me here alone. I hear the door slam closed, the lock sliding clunkily into place.

I'm going to die here.

No. I'm not going to give up yet. There has to be something I can do, something I can use, to get me out of this. My only real option is to get free and try to break down the door. Now Forra is no longer here, I use my strength to try and sever the cuffs holding my wrists and ankles together. With one swift tug, I manage to break the cuffs off my wrists, and now, having my hands free, I make quick work of my ankle cuffs. Should I have done this when Forra was here? I mentally kick myself for not at least trying. However, I have no idea what skill set she has, so it may have been too big of a risk. Honestly, it didn't cross my mind. She made me feel helpless and so I believed I was.

I glance around for something to use on the door. It looks pretty sturdy, so I don't think I'll be able to kick it down, but perhaps I could break the lock with something? I find absolutely nothing. The metal pipe I was strapped to is set into the roof with concrete, and I can't see anything else I can use. I do try breaking down the door with some hard kicks, but it's useless.

Panic starts to rise within me again, as the reality of my situation dawns on me. I'm alone, no one knows I'm here so there's no rescue coming, and I'm going to die from heat exhaustion. How long will it be before my family and friends learn that I died? How much is this going to hurt?

I take a moment to calm myself down, taking deep breaths as panic leads to further panic, and come up with a plan. All the buildings around me are shorter than the one I'm on, so no one can see me. Leaning over the roof's edge, I see if I could possibly make the jump to the nearest building, but it's far beyond what I'm comfortable with. I shout for help for a few minutes and try kicking the locked door again, but I don't even leave a mark with my shoe, let alone dent it.

I'm truly stuck.

I take another look at the nearest building and see it has a narrow flagpole near the side. The memory of Kriger catching me when I fell from one mere weeks ago surges up, but I quickly quash it back down. All my memories of our time together have been thoroughly tainted by his betrayal.

If I could somehow get the pole to bend my way, then there's a chance I could make it onto the next roof. I can see from here that the roof door on that building is propped open, so it's my best shot, but I've never managed to use my Tk for anything remotely that big before.

Forra's words swim into my mind. I can't believe my mother crippled me with limited Tk when I could be so much stronger. I mean, if what Forra said was true, then I'm sure being pregnant with a strongly Telekinetic baby must have been a challenge. But surely my mum would have let me have my full power back before I turned two, at least. I would have found it hard to control my Tk, but she could have taught me. If she was planning on lifting the restriction when I was older, maybe there's something I could do to lift it now? In the past, whenever I've tried pushing through the pain, I've given up. The pain is always so bad, it has never been worth forcing myself to continue. Today, I'm going to put everything I have into it; I've got to try.

Standing near the edge of the roof, but not too close, in case I collapse, I reach out with my mind and pull.

Nothing happens. The flagpole doesn't even wobble.

I pull harder. The pain is already there behind my right eye. As I continue to pull, the pain grows, reaching around my eye and back to the base of my skull. I can't help but growl and then scream as the pain becomes too much to bear. Tears roll down my cheeks, my vision becomes hazy, but still I pull. I fall to my knees. I don't have much left in me; I can't even see out of my right eye anymore.

And then nothing.

The pain is gone, and I hear a loud thud beneath me.

Did I die? It's a weird thought, but it takes me a second to take stock of what's happened. I'm kneeling on the ground, I can see out of my right eye again, and the pain has gone. I want to laugh in relief, but the urgency of my situation takes over. I scoot forward and lean over the edge of the building to see what the noise was.

It was the flagpole. It's now resting against my building, a couple of feet below the roof. Close enough that I can lower myself onto it and slide across to the next building. Did I really do that?

I look around for something to test my Tk on again and spy a large metal barrel on the building opposite. I reach out and brace for the pain, but it never comes. The barrel sails across the roof and hits the small wall at the side of the building.

I can't believe it.

I don't have much time to dwell on this; I need to get off this building and into the cool shade of the stairwell opposite. There's only the small matter of sliding along this flagpole, with at least a fifty-storey drop below me. No biggy. I don't want to think about this for much longer; best to get it over with as fast as possible.

I ease myself over the edge of the building and a gust of wind tugs at my legs. I hold still for a second, to let it pass, then lower myself onto the pole. I slowly allow my full weight onto it, to check it can take me, before releasing my grip from the side of the building.

I start to shimmy my way down, but then another large gust of wind whips between the two buildings, causing me to lose my balance. My whole body swings around and underneath the pole, making me scream. Now I only have the strength of my arms and legs to stop me from falling. I do my best not to look down and make quick work of getting to the base of the pole on the opposite building.

It's not until I make it up and over the wall that I fully realise how close I came to dying. The metal pole has partially sheared off at the base. One more jolt and it would have come away completely.

I want to throw up, again, but swallow the bile back down and make a run for the open door.

CHAPTER 14

My feet pound the stairs as I make my way down; I really hope the door is unlocked at the bottom. Do I need to be quiet? I want to be outside and not trapped in a metal tube, so I don't try to soften my footsteps. I'm so relieved to be out of the sun; the almost frigid, air-conditioned air kisses my skin, and I pull up my sleeves to cool myself further. My breath comes faster and my heart pounds from the exertion and adrenaline. I want to take a break, I desperately need water, but I dare not stop for even a moment.

Many minutes pass before I find myself at the bottom. Please don't tell me I went too far and am now in the basement. The door in front of me is, blessedly, unlocked. I silently ease it open and peer out. There's an open foyer in front of me, but no one in sight. I take my chances and make a run for the glass doors. The first one I tug at is locked; I rapidly try all the doors until, finally, I manage to pull the last one open. I run out into a wall of heat, then move around the side of the building, before allowing myself to pause and catch my breath.

Oh boy, it is even hotter out here than up on the roof. The heat reflecting from the pavements makes it feel like I'm in a sauna. There's at least some shade between these buildings, so I risk rolling up my jeans and exposing some skin to help keep me cool. I look around and can't help but notice how clean everything is. There are trees everywhere, although there is something slightly odd about them, and all the buildings are made out of… yellow sandstone? I'm not sure, but the uniformity of the buildings only adds to the sense of cleanliness.

I make my way over to one of the trees nearest to me, to get a closer look, and discover that it's not real. In fact, none of these trees are real. It dawns on me, from the research I did back at the Academy, that I must be inside a major city's walls, where they have manufactured flora and fauna. To compensate for the depletion of many of their natural resources over millennia, from all the alien invasions, they were offered technology in exchange.

There's an almost imperceptible hiss, then blessedly cold air wafts down from the top of the tree. It lands on my face and, for a mere moment, I feel cool relief. I don't want to stay here too long contemplating the trees; I need to get far away from these buildings, and, hopefully, Forra.

I head towards a park I can see that's a short walk away. There appears to be lots of people milling about there, so I hope I'll be able to blend in and come up with a plan.

Entering the park, I spot a drinking water fountain, which I make quick work of before really taking in my surroundings. The park is stunning, with an array of colours and water features, but it's so strange how everything is mechanised. The trees are very convincing, until you get up close and realise they're actually beautifully crafted metal. There's plenty of cool air wafting down around me, so it's almost pleasant to walk outside here. I hear a slight squeak and look at my right shoulder to see a metal butterfly sitting there. Its wings could do with a dab of oil.

People keep giving me strange looks. I'm not sure if it's because they're able to read my mind – quite likely on Malam

– or because I'm not dressed nearly as smartly as they are. As I walk through the park and gather my thoughts, I realise I'm drawing more and more attention to myself, which is the last thing I want to do. So, instead, I decide to head straight for their Rip and hope I'll be able to explain my situation to someone and make it home. I know Forra has friends that helped her, but I can't believe that's the case for most of the people working there. I really ought to try this as soon as possible because, when Forra realises I've left, that's the first place she'll look.

Approaching an elderly couple, hoping they've got the time to speak to me, I ask the way to the Rip. They look alarmed when I start a conversation, but they do at least, begrudgingly, confirm they understand my language, and quickly point out the way to the Rip. I think they wanted to have as little to do with me as possible, and that was likely the quickest way to get rid of me. Thanking them profusely, I head off in the direction they indicated, vastly relieved to discover it's not only in this city, but merely a few streets away. I quicken my pace, exiting the park and making my way along a highway. The air is hotter here, but I don't really care. I'm purely focused on getting home.

I'm rehearsing what I'm going to say to the guardians when I turn a corner and spot the, very large, guardian symbol on the side of a red-brick building. It stands out like a sore thumb amongst the endless sea of sandstone. I hurry up the steps and am met in the reception area by an incredibly tall and muscular woman. She smiles calmly down at me, but then her eyes quickly narrow as she takes a closer look. I feel a slight tingling in my mind, so I'm pretty sure she's reading my thoughts. I try to lock them down – although I've had no practice with this – but everything is so raw, it's pretty impossible to do.

"Welcome to the Rip," she says, in English. "How may I be

of assistance?"

"I need to get back home. It's an emergency," I reply, breathlessly.

"I see," she replies, primly, then proceeds to type at length into the computer in front of her.

Panic starts to rise within me again. I don't want to stand here talking to her, I want to be on the other side of security. I feel so exposed, and I would really like to know what she's typing.

"Okay, so it might be possible to get you across, but as you haven't booked passage, and I don't see a record of anyone your age having come here recently, we will need to interview you first."

"That's absolutely fine," I reply, relief clear in my voice. "I can explain exactly how that happened."

The tension and fear that's been keeping me going starts to ebb away, replaced by utter exhaustion. I sag into her desk and spot two burly guardians walking in my direction. One of whom has a distinct smirk on his face, sending a shot of unease down my spine. This does not feel right. I don't think they intend for me to have any type of interview; these men don't look like they'll let me leave. Without a backwards glance, I turn and run for the doors. Thankfully, one door to the side is propped open, so I don't waste any time getting out of there.

I hear shouts go up behind me, and the sound of weapons charging up, but I ignore it and focus on my speed. I try weaving a little before I can duck down a side street, anything to keep me alive and moving. Many Malamborn don't have speed and strength in their DNA, but they do have telepathy and insane technology. They'll be able to track me through their extensive digital surveillance network and then communicate with guardians on the ground instantly. I need to get out of this city.

I spot the wall surrounding the city in the distance and decide that it's my only chance to get away. I've heard there isn't as much security outside the major cities, as it's where people without money, or telepathic ability, live. Even if they discover I've crossed over, it should be harder for them to find me. Forra will surely have been alerted by now as to my disappearance, so she'll be on the hunt too.

I follow one of the roads heading towards the wall; there has to be an exit point at the end of it. I can't hear anyone following me now, but I don't slow down; they could appear at any moment. The wall appears directly in front of me and is insanely high. There is no way I can jump over it, and it's too smooth to climb. Every car that passes through the gates is checked thoroughly by guards, so I can't sneak by without drawing attention. It's likely they've already been alerted about my escape, so I don't have many options.

I pause for a few seconds to gather my thoughts and hear sirens in the distance. They might not be for me, but I can't delay further and take that chance. I have to get to the other side of the wall, by whatever means necessary.

Decision made, I run for it. I leap over the roofs of the vehicles in front of me, there's not enough room to go around, and use my newly discovered Tk to widen the gates enough so I can pass through. Not having experience with my stronger Tk, I massively underestimate my power, and the gates fly off their hinges. The sound is immense, and people are shouting and beeping their horns. I don't even glance behind me but use the confusion to my advantage and launch myself through the newly widened opening. I hear engines starting up, but I'm pretty confident I can find somewhere to hide.

The putrid smells of the dirty streets hit me, a sharp contrast to the pristine ones I've left behind. The buildings are shorter and less well-ordered than the inner city, giving the place a very haphazard feel. I pass a few abandoned buildings and decide to sneak into one, to give myself a break before I come up with my next plan of action.

I slip through an open window into a dark and dingy room. The smell of rotting rubbish fills my nose, and I have to breathe through my mouth to stop myself from gagging. It's seriously foul. Although the sun is still high in the sky, it's relatively dark and cool in here. With all the buildings so close together, the streets are more sheltered and, thankfully, a lot colder. I stand to the side of the window, so no one can spot me if they pass by, but also so I can still look out. I hear some vehicles revving in the distance, but otherwise I can't hear anything suspicious. I'm sure Forra and some of her friends will be here soon, but for the moment, I feel relatively safe.

So, what now? I can't go back through the Rip without help. Money talks here, so maybe I could get some and bribe someone. Do my dad and friends have any idea what's happened? How long have I been here? It might not have even been twenty-four hours since I was taken, so they may not yet have noticed I'm missing.

I feel a sharp pang of homesickness in my chest. What I wouldn't give right now to be back at home with Dad berating me about joining the Academy. The adrenaline I was working off has deserted my body, and all I'm left with is exhaustion. I'm too tired even to panic. I need food, oh gosh, I desperately need food, and money. Maybe I could find someone willing to employ me? Preferably doing something that doesn't involve working outside, exposing myself to the heat and watchful eyes.

The streets around here appear quiet, so I take a more thorough peep through the window to get my bearings. Most of the buildings nearby appear to be empty, and the wall, still visible due to its immense size, is reassuringly far away. My eyes do land on one building at the end of the street that seems to be occupied. There are a couple of people milling around it, and there's a glowing neon sign. I'm too far down the street to read what it says, but decide to check it out. Maybe it's a shop where I could work for food.

I approach quietly, keeping myself pressed to the side of the building, in case I need to make a discreet exit. The men clustered close to the entrance don't seem to be aware of the skulking teenage girl approaching them. I glance up at the sign, but it's written in a language I don't understand. However, there's also a smaller sign written in English. Well, approximately. Lots of worlds developed their own languages, but there are quite a few where they speak something similar to English, so it's often widely used. From what I can make out, this appears to be some sort of bar where people place bets on fights. No idea if it's people or chickens who do the fighting.

As I edge closer to the door, doing my best to ignore the looks of the men nearby, I can hear the sounds of fists hitting flesh. So, I'm guessing the fights take place on the premises and that it's definitely people who do the fighting. There don't appear to be any other establishments nearby, and the last thing I want is to ask for work in a more reputable place that may report me to the guardians. Decision made, I ease my way in through the single door to the dusky room inside.

Smoke permeates the air around me. The smell is odd though; it's certainly not regular cigarettes being smoked here. I turn my attention to the raised fighting ring at one end of the room and see two tall men doing their best to knock each other out. Or, at least, I hope that's all they're trying to do. They don't have any weapons, or really any technique, but brute strength seems to be the winning factor here. I could definitely take them, if needed. I somehow doubt I'd be allowed to fight, but it's tempting to ask. It's certainly a skill I have. I imagine the fighters are paid fairly well, certainly better than someone washing the cups at the end of the night. I decide, perhaps foolishly, to go for it.

I try to push some confidence into my stride as I make my way to the bar. Doing my best to lock down my thoughts, as I figure I'm going to, at least, have to lie about my age, I approach the young man behind the bar. Tall with dark skin and beautiful eyelashes, which I can spot from a few paces away, he looks too gorgeous to be working in a place like this.

He looks up, somewhat startled to see me, and gives me the once-over before asking me something in the local dialect. Seeing my obvious confusion, not to mention my relatively short stature and very pale appearance – neither of which is common here on Malam – he switches to a more common tongue.

"I said: you lost?"

"Um, no? I want to fight."

He just smiles at this, clearly thinking I'm joking. I merely raise an eyebrow, pointedly, and wait.

His smile drops. "No, you are young and female."

"So? I'm eighteen," I lie, "and I can easily fight those two there." I gesture behind me at the two buffoons in the ring. I feel the now familiar tingle in my mind, and quickly quiet my thoughts. Instead, I try and think of all those times I've successfully beaten Kriger in training and hope the man can see I'm serious and not underage. Although, I have no idea what the legal ages are for things here.

The man's eyebrows creep up towards his hairline, and the soft tingle in my mind departs with a whisper of… mint? Weird, I didn't know the mind could smell of something. I file that away to research later.

"We don't have females, but we could change," he says thoughtfully.

His 'English' is pretty good, if a little stilted, but his accent makes it sound decadent. I can feel myself being drawn to him slightly and have to give myself a mental shake. For all I know, he's somehow manipulating me to like him. I need to keep my guard up.

"Change sounds good," I reply. "Does it pay well?" I have no idea about the currency here, so anything would be good, but I don't want to reveal that.

"Yes." He nods. "Money for fight and more money if you win."

Well, okay then.

I nod in agreement. "How do I get started?"

"First, you fight Jam, and then we see."

"Jam?" That has to be a name and not a condiment.

The man points to the very tall and muscular man standing to the side of the ring.

Oh. That's Jam. "Uh, okay. And your name?" I ask. I should at least know the name of the man who's sending me to my doom.

"Reyta," he tells me.

Huh, pretty.

I nod, and head over to Jam after some encouragement from Reyta.

Jam is even taller close up. I crane my neck upwards to speak to him, as he looms over me. "Uh, hi? I'm to fight you, Reyta told me," I say, pointing at a smiling Reyta behind me.

"Okay," Jam replies, and then turns away from me to enter the now vacated ring.

Oh right, we're fighting now. I clench my fists a few times, give myself a mental pep talk, and then slide between the ropes and into the – ew, sticky – ring. I really hope that's sweat and not blood. Hard to tell on a black floor. I'm guessing that's why they painted it black. Jam is far bigger than anyone I've fought before, but as long as he doesn't have any surprising talents, I'm pretty sure I have a shot at winning here.

Jam doesn't waste any time and takes a swing at my head. I easily duck away, and dance around him. He's slow to turn but that fist came fast, so I won't underestimate him. He growls slightly, to intimidate, and takes another swing. This time going for an uppercut, which I dodge with ease. Being fast is really going to help. No idea if I'm stronger, but I should be strong enough to knock him out. I don't want to get too close for any length of time, as his arm reach is extensive, and if he grabs me, he'll be near impossible to shake off. I aim low and try to sweep his legs out from under him; a man this size could knock himself out if he fell hard enough. He skilfully avoids my attempt and gives me a sneer for good measure.

Out of the corner of my eye, I catch Reyta looking bored, with his arms folded across his chest. Clearly, I'm not showing him what I'm capable of. I decide not to waste my time dodging but to go for a sharp strike to end this. And I do. With a swift left hook, people so rarely watch the left-hand side, I catch Jam at the base of his jaw. His head snaps back and to the side, a look of shock passing over his features, before he drops unconscious to the floor.

The sound of slow clapping from behind has me turning to

see an approving look on Reyta's face.

"That will work," he says. "Do you have home, clothes or food?"

I shake my head, not quite sure if this is a requirement for the job.

"Fine, head through that door." He gestures to an almost camouflaged door behind the ring – everything is painted black here. "Find Olla, she will help."

"Um, okay, thanks." I give him a nod and make a beeline for the door. I don't want to be around when Jam wakes up. I have a feeling I won't be his favourite person for a while.

I head through the back door and am immediately assaulted by the smell of perfume and hairspray. I look around and find a tall, statuesque woman rummaging through a box of scarves. This must be Olla.

"Olla?" I ask. The woman in question turns towards me with a raised eyebrow. "Reyta said to come speak to you. I'm to fight in the ring, but don't have clothes, food or a home." Man, I sound pathetic and desperate. Well, I'm certainly the latter.

"Okay. Why?"

"Why what?"

"Why do you have no home or money?"

I decide to go for honesty here. I have a sense Olla can smell, or perhaps read, a lie from twenty paces. "I'm hiding and trying to get back home. People are after me, and I think they want to kill me."

"Did you hurt or steal from someone?"

"No, never. They are not good people."

"Okay, I understand. Come, we will make you look show-ready, and perhaps a bit different from what people are expecting you to look like, hm?"

191

"Oh, yes please. Thank you so much." The rush of gratitude I feel towards this young woman is overwhelming. I actually jump forward and give her a hug, a rare thing for me to do at the best of times. I'm so relieved to have found someone so readily able to help; the past few hours have been a tad trying.

Olla merely smiles quietly, disentangles my arms from around her, and gets straight to work.

Three hours later, I look like a completely different person. I've discovered Olla is in charge of the interval entertainment. Essentially, her and a few other girls parade around and take the bets from the crowd between fights. So, she has a lot of costumes, makeup and hair dye. Olla has cut my hair, which was a little painful to watch, and it's now sitting a mere centimetre below my chin. Oh, and she died it dark red. The outfit she found for me is perfect: super stretchy black leggings and a sleeveless vest. The vest even has a little padding to absorb some punches. Hopefully, I won't be needing that.

I'm standing in the small room that will be my bedroom. It's above the bar and has only a bed and a sink inside. Reyta has promised me more food from the bar and has already given me a little money to get me started. Although, I have yet to learn the value of this currency. It appears that having a female fighter, particularly one as young as me, is quite unusual. Reyta was practically gleaming at the number of bets already placed, once word got out. I'm a little apprehensive that the wrong people will hear about this, but at least I'll be able to make some money quite quickly.

I can hear the crowd downstairs chatting and clinking their

bottles. I'm to fight the winner of the previous fight, around halfway through the night. I'm already exhausted, as I haven't laid down since I woke up on that roof. But the adrenaline for the fight ahead is really helping to keep me going. I hear a thud and then a resounding cheer as someone else has been knocked out. Only one more fight to go. I decide to head down and, as discreetly as I can, watch this fight. I want to get a good idea of who I'm up against.

Huh, one of the guys is nothing like I expected. He's tall, everyone is tall here, but very lithe. Not at all like the other fighters, who look like they can walk through walls. As I watch him fight, I can see how fast he is. This should be interesting. I should be worried, or at the very least concerned, but I'm genuinely excited. I've got a lot of frustration and anxiety to burn, and there's nothing like letting go in a fight. His opponent is clearly not going to win: he may be big but he's practically stumbling around the ring.

A few moments later, Big And Stumbly crashes to the ground in a heap of muscles. It's an almost comical sight. His body is swiftly dragged out of the ring, nine men were needed, and then Olla and her gang come out to start collecting the last bets.

Reyta jumps up into the ring to make an announcement. I don't understand the words, but I do hear my name, or at least the one I gave, 'Blue', and head towards the ring. The punters swiftly spot me and part to give me a small path, so I can make my way up. My opponent in the ring leans against the ropes and leers at me. Nice. Jam appears at my side and helps me into the ring. I didn't really need him to do that, but I appreciate the support. He gives me a brief wink before letting go of my hand.

I guess there are no hard feelings. I give him a quick smile in return, before turning to face my opponent.

I stand tall, feeling many eyes upon me. They're shouting something, and I think it's directed at me, but I have no idea what they're saying. Perhaps it's for the best.

Reyta points to me and shouts, "Blue!" and then to the guy "Rinor!"

I'm guessing that's his name then.

Reyta slaps the ground with his hand, and it's begun. Rinor moves swiftly around me but doesn't attempt a strike. I don't either. We're both sizing each other up, trying to find a weakness or perhaps a tell that lets us know when the other is about to attack. I focus on Rinor's legs, they're usually the first to show intention. A mere twitch of the thigh can divulge which arm or leg is about to be launched. He gives away nothing, only showing me that smirk, which seems permanently plastered to his face. I try not to demonstrate how fast I am. As my best bet here is to catch him off guard, I need to strike first.

I jump into his space with a quick jab to the base of his neck, before quickly leaping back. I make contact, but in my haste, I used minimal strength, so he barely gags in response. He's glowering at me now, and aims a strike at my head, which I dodge with ease. I repeat the exercise of jumping in and out, to see if he responds in the same way again. He does, only this time with a little less care. He's clearly irritated, and his strikes are becoming less controlled.

I repeat this a few more times before changing it up for a sweep of the legs. He was so focused on my arms he didn't see it coming. He falls flat on his back, the air whooshing from his lungs, and I'm on him before he can bounce back up. I leap onto his chest, my knees braced on his shoulders, and deliver a hard blow to the side of his head. He's out but still breathing.

The roar from the crowd makes my ears ring. I cringe, having honestly forgotten about them as I was so focused on fighting. I glance up at Reyta as he enters the ring to congratulate me. I stand next to him, staring blindly at the people before me.

I enjoyed that but really wish we didn't have to knock our opponent unconscious in order to win. What if I strike too hard one time? That thought sends a wave of nausea over me, but I quickly clamp it back down. I need the money, and I need to get home to stop whatever Forra is up to.

I have to fight twice more before Reyta ends the night. He promises me that I won't need to fight from the beginning every night. He likes to save his stronger fighters till the end, as it keeps the customers wanting more. I'm exhausted and head straight to bed, with a plate of food in hand, of course. I really want to pass out and forget this day ever happened.

A week passes, or at least I think it does, the days and nights merge into one here. I haven't left the premises for fear I'll be spotted, although I look so different now, it'd take a trained eye to recognise me. The bruises on my arms and legs, not to mention my hands and torso, glare back at me with their sickly purple and green colouring. My pale skin merely highlighting where I misjudged my opponent. I haven't lost a fight yet, although I have been close several times.

I've developed quite a following amongst some of the regulars and have been receiving gifts, and one or two proposals. I am quite partial to the sweet pastries a few have been sending. I never reply, as I certainly don't wish to encourage anyone, but the extra calories have been very welcome. It is a concern, however, that I am making such a splash here. I have a dreadful feeling the wrong person will come and investigate what all the fuss is about and take me back to Forra. Olla has been my gatekeeper, and I'm indebted to her for all her help. I share many of my gifts with her and the other girls, and, in turn, they make sure no one else gets close to me.

Tonight's fight is like any other, until I enter the bar. There is an increased tension in the air, the crowd feels more ramped up than usual. I can't put my finger on it, but something feels off. I look up at the ring and spot Rinor fighting again. I sigh, he's likely to win this and then it'll be the two of us again. It'll be the third time we've fought this week.

Mere moments later, we're in the ring and dancing around each other. I'm tired, and impatient, so I don't make a show of it. Instead, I strike swiftly and true, nearly my full force behind it. Rinor goes flying across the ring and lands with a dull thud. The crowd holds its collective breath, whilst one of the girls checks him over, before giving the okay. The sound erupts around me. Normally, they'd want more of a show, but having a slight girl take down an impressive fighter so quickly sits well with them. I'm relieved. Only one more fight left tonight, and then I can retreat to the safety of my room.

Reyta jumps in and announces the name of the next fighter. It's a name I haven't heard before, so I look over to the parting crowd to see who it is. A familiar outline moves towards the ring, a hood drawn up over their head, and slides between the ropes to face me. My heart is racing: I know him. The man lowers his hood and reveals his face.

Kriger.

CHAPTER 15

I stare, shocked, into those vivid green eyes. They're inspecting me thoroughly, as if to make sure I'm real. I can't believe he is here, how is he here? A thousand questions whir through my mind, mixed with the feeling of betrayal. One thought cuts through the rest: he's here to take me back to Forra.

I can't let that happen.

Reyta drops his hand to the floor and the fight is on. I know how to best Kriger, months of practise have honed my skills. However, he likely feels the same way about fighting me. He lands a few dummy punches towards me to draw me in, but he's slower than usual. Maybe the heat has got to him. I don't fall for his traps and keep moving, making him turn to keep me in sight. If I can knock him out, then I could make a run for it. I've got some of my money on me for such an occasion; it might be enough to get me home.

I spot an opening and strike. He dodges and my fist brushes past his cheek. His eyes widen in surprise. I've bested him a few times before, so this shouldn't be unusual. His eyes seem to be trying to convey something. He's looking at me earnestly. Surely, Forra has told him I know the truth about his betrayal. So why does he look so concerned?

The fight continues for several minutes, neither of us managing to land any blows. I'm more confused than ever, as he's not behaving in a way I'd expect someone in his position to. Whilst I'm distracted trying to put all the pieces of this puzzle together, he makes an unorthodox move. He leaps forwards, wraps his arms around me, and takes us both down to the sticky ground. The weight of him expels a breath from my lungs. I'm instantly aware of his body pressed against mine. I mentally give myself a kick; my body seems to have forgotten that we hate Kriger now. I try to wriggle free, but he leans in close.

He whispers, "Don't knock me out. Hold back your punch and I'll pretend to go down. I'll meet you outside after."

I shove my face towards his as I continue to struggle. "So you can kidnap me?"

He looks shocked. "No, so I can rescue you."

His grip loosens and I wriggle free with a shove. So he can rescue me? Is this some kind of sick joke?

I scramble to my feet, and back into a fighting stance. I glance across at Kriger. He looks so honest and solemn that I'm beginning to think I might have things the wrong way around. I really don't want to knock him out; the feelings I had for him before are still there. I decide to go along with his idea. It's a risk, but my plan is taking too long anyway. Besides, if he does mean me harm, he likely would have kidnapped me already.

We dance around for another minute before he leaves a rather obvious – to the trained eye – opening, and I take it. Kriger drops down onto the ground, eyes closed, and really does look to be out for the count. A flicker of regret runs through me. I might have made it a little too convincing.

Reyta jumps back in, once Olla has confirmed the end of the fight, and I make a discreet exit. I wave to the other girls as I pass them, grab a few personal items – and the rest of my money – from my room, and head towards the back door.

"You're leaving?"

I turn to find Olla standing a few feet away from me.

"You never go outside."

I'm not sure how much to tell her, so I decide to go for the truth – sort of. "There's a friend I need to meet. If I don't come back, please don't worry. I'm hopeful it's good news." Not giving her the chance to reply, I give her a swift firm hug. "Thank you for everything. You have no idea what your kindness has meant to me."

I open the door, turning once to give her a final smile before leaving. Olla looks surprised, but she merely shrugs her shoulders and gives me a wave, then gets back to work.

I find a quiet side street and watch the bar, waiting for Kriger. It's not long before he makes his appearance. Once he's outside, I step into view so he can spot me, then return to my hiding place. Kriger takes a few furtive glances around before jogging over to see me.

He immediately wraps me in a bear hug. I stand stiffly in his arms for a few beats, before returning it. I've only been gone a week, but it seems like a lot longer, and the feel of Kriger's arms around me is the comfort I've been craving.

"Are you okay?" he asks, releasing me from his hug and giving me a thorough inspection. He frowns at the bruises lining my arms.

At least it's pretty obvious where I got those.

"I think so. But what on earth are you doing here? Last I heard, it was you who betrayed me to Jed, and possibly Ivy, which allowed Forra to kidnap me and take me here."

"What?" he whisper-shouts. "Is that what she said?"

"Well, not exactly. Only that someone from my team betrayed me, someone who I've grown close with. What else was I to think?" I'm starting to feel a little defensive. I don't like how quickly I believed the worst of him.

"It wasn't me. It was Ashleigh."

"Ashleigh?" I practically squeak. "But why?"

"That's her own story to tell. Basically, she had her reasons, but she's on our side now."

Kriger's hands are still gripping my shoulders, his thumbs gently caressing me.

"How did you find me, and how on earth did you get here? Are you alone?"

"No, Merk and Connor are with me."

"Connor? How did he get away from Ivy?"

"It's a long story, and I promise I'll fill you in soon, but we need to get out of here, to somewhere safer."

He grabs my hand and pulls me down the alley, before glancing back at me with a small, private smile.

"By the way," he says, "I like your hair."

My heart gives a little flip, and then we're diving into the dark.

Kriger seems to know his way around. We weave through the shadowy streets, pausing occasionally to check that we remain unseen. It takes a full ten minutes, but then Kriger tugs me into a small room in a deserted house.

"We should be safe now for a little while. Merk and Connor are due to meet me here shortly."

"How do you know your way around so well? Have you been here long?"

"Three days. We've been trying to get your attention, hoping that you got our messages to meet, but I don't think you ever did."

"Messages?"

"Yeah, we sent gifts to Blue with messages in the cards. We kept them vague enough to be safe, but thought you'd understand."

"I never received them. Olla, one of the girls, she always checks what the girls and I receive, in case it's anything dangerous."

It's so strange to think some of those gifts were from Kriger, but with the notes removed. I feel the protective wall I placed around my heart start to crumble.

"So, tell me everything," I plead. "Is Ivy definitely part of this then?"

"Yes, she is, although we don't have enough evidence yet to take to the council. Forra is the only one who knows Ivy's true involvement. Fram and Merk, with a little help from Ashleigh and I, were able to get Connor out. They really were not keeping him that securely."

Kriger runs a hand through his already mussed-up hair. He looks exhausted, he's probably not had a good night's sleep all week. Guilt nags at me because I've had a proper room with a bed and food for a while now.

"If they weren't keeping him securely locked up, then perhaps they're tracking him to try and incriminate him further, along with those working with him."

"That's what we think too, although Connor has been using his ability to create a null space fairly regularly, to prevent any electronic surveillance. Anyway, your rescue was too big a priority, we'll deal with the fallout when we're back on Earth. We might need to hide on Evig for a while though; Ivy and

Forra have a lot of friends."

I shiver in response. The thought of being back home throws up many mixed feelings. I long to see my dad and hang out with Cassie, and I really miss my bed, but I absolutely don't want to put them in any more danger.

"Does my dad know what's going on? He's going to seriously freak out about all this."

"Don't worry, Fram fed him some rubbish about a spontaneous training exercise that only works if you have no prior warning. Your dad was satisfied with that answer, although Fram said he looked far from happy."

"Yeah, my dad hates that I'm training to work in the role that got my mother killed. But at least I can now tell him how she died and why." I proceed to give Kriger a full rundown of what happened with Forra, and my subsequent escape. His eyebrows could not creep up any higher, especially when I tell him about my new level of Tk.

"Wow, Indie, that's completely insane. Not the family reunion you were hoping for, but I'm really happy to hear your Tk no longer hurts you." He runs a hand over my hair. "Have you been experimenting with it?"

"Actually, I haven't really tried much. Forra said it's hard to control, which has been my experience so far, and I've been trying to keep a low profile."

"That makes sense."

Silence enters the room between us. The small space feels even more cramped all of a sudden. I look up into Kriger's face. He stares back intently, and reaches to pull my face towards his. I tilt my head back to receive his kiss.

There's a noise at the entrance of the building.

Kriger and I immediately tense and jump apart; our lips

hadn't even touched. He quickly shoves me behind him, gripping my wrist gently to keep me in place. He's so broad I can barely see around his shoulder. If this is Merk or Connor, maybe they should come up with some kind of secret knock?

Connor's head peeks around the door.

"Maybe we should come up with a secret knock?" Kriger suggests.

Huh? Great minds…

"Indigo?" Connor asks. "You got her alright then?"

"Not without a fight." Kriger turns and gives me a knowing smile.

"Good," says Merk, entering the cramped space, "time to put our escape plan into action."

"So, there is a plan to get us all out then?" I look expectantly at the three of them.

Connor chuckles, actually chuckles.

"Of course, Indigo, although you might not be very happy about it."

I'm staring at a suitcase Merk has wheeled in. They have got to be kidding me. "You can't be serious. No one is going to fall for that."

"Of course not. It's merely step one."

Connor proceeds to explain that they're going to use the case to smuggle me back into the city, but I won't be in it when crossing through the Rip. They've been bribing everyone they could get their hands on to help us all get home safely. Connor can disrupt the security cameras that are close in range, so I'll be able to extract myself from the case before we enter the building for Rip transport. Merk is very happy I've already dyed my hair, so he passes me a set of clear, thick-rimmed glasses to disguise me further. I've got a fake name and pass for the Rip, although anyone loyal to Forra will know that the unknown girl travelling with Earth and Evig nationals has to be me. Connor tells me we have a set time to enter the building, which will be when the people who they've managed to bribe are working.

It's far from a foolproof plan, but staying on Malam any longer only increases our chances of discovery. The three of them stare at me expectantly.

"Oh, you want me to get in the suitcase now?"

Kriger shifts about on his feet, clearly uncomfortable with all this.

As I contort my body into the case, doing my best to cover myself with the few items of clothing, Kriger bends down towards me.

"I promise we'll get you out of here," he whispers.

He kisses me lightly on the cheek, before covering me with a layer of clothes. Darkness envelops me as the case is zipped shut, and the hard edges dig into my sides. Thankfully they left a small gap in the zip, so I'm not too concerned about suffocating. It's a really good thing I'm not claustrophobic.

The case is then pulled upright, and I slide down towards my feet, so I'm in a crouched position. It's actually a lot more comfortable like this. I immediately regret that thought as they drag the case along the rough streets. I try to take some calming breaths, anything to slow my heartrate and distract me from what we're about to do. This is seriously crazy.

From what I can tell, I've been gently placed inside a car and am now being driven towards a gate in the wall surrounding the city. I can't hear anything over the rumble of the engine and the sound of the tyres on the rough road. Even when we stop at a checkpoint, or at least I think it's a checkpoint, I still cannot hear anything. That is, until the boot opens.

I stay absolutely still, assuming that someone's checking what Connor and the guys are taking through into the city. Voices speak, but in a language I don't recognise. Holding my breath, my only hope is that no one looks inside the suitcase. I'm pretty well covered by the clothes, but one rummage through and it's all over.

The sound of the zipper moving causes my heart to go into overdrive. The noise feels deafening in my cocoon. I ready myself to fight; they're certainly going to discover me. Cooler air enters the case as the lid is lifted, but I dare not breathe it in. People are speaking, one of them is Merk, and they're both speaking the local language. Laughter erupts between them, so maybe this is someone they bribed? Gosh, I hope so.

The minutes stretch out, until the darkness of the suitcase surrounds me once more. The zipper and boot are closed, and we're on the move. I take a deep shuddery breath; I can't believe we made it through. Relief washes over me, but it's short lived, as that was merely step one.

The drive from the checkpoint only takes a few minutes, but we've taken so many turns that I've completely lost my sense of direction. The car stops, and I feel the doors slamming closed as the guys get out. The boot is finally opened again, and I'm released from my prison. I tumble out of the suitcase and Kriger is immediately there, lifting me back onto my feet and checking me over. He runs a hand through my dishevelled hair, then passes me a chocolate bar. It's a Venus bar from back home. The sight of it nearly brings tears to my eyes, but I devour it instead. Chocolate and caramel melt on my tongue as I close my eyes and relish the taste of home. I open them to see Kriger staring, rather intently, at my mouth. I'm immediately self-conscious, but he catches my eye and smirks, before turning his attention to Merk and Connor.

"Right, Indigo," says Merk, "we've only got half an hour to wait before the shifts change. Connor should be able to keep us digitally undetected for that long. Afterwards, we need to all walk confidently and calmly to the Rip's building." He rummages around in his back pocket and passes me a bunch of papers. "Here are your new, temporary, ID cards. You're still listed as a trainee guardian, as you have the tattoo, and it also explains to any innocent parties why you would be here with two fully trained guardians. As far as anyone is concerned, we were here on a small expedition to learn about other worlds. Always best not to complicate things."

He seems quietly chuffed with himself and, I have to say, I'm impressed. The photo they have on the card is me, but with blonde hair. Can't say I'm a fan of the look. However, it all appears genuine, and my name is now Tatiana Armitage. Nice.

The wait is excruciating. Not least because of the heat. I keep myself pressed up against the wall, to stay in the shade and out of sight of passers-by. Unfortunately, there are no artificial trees on this street releasing their cool air. Connor questions me incessantly; he seems really interested in the block that was placed on my Tk. Sounds like, all being well, I've got a lot of training sessions lined up for me in the future.

Connor and Merk are also very curious to hear what Forra has told me. They were both completely blindsided when they heard it was Forra who betrayed their group. She was, apparently, the one who was most upset by the loss of Elna, so it was very hard for them to believe she had anything to do with it. Connor assumes she must have been very careful when talking to him because he would have been able to spot her lies.

They tell me about the fallout from my mother's death, and how sorry they are that they weren't able to prevent it. It's clear that, although it happened a long time ago, it's still very raw for them. It's hard to listen to them recount everything, but I absorb every detail they give about my mother, particularly about her temperament. She sounds a lot like me.

The conversation moves onto my time as a fighter at the bar. I don't mind all the questions though; they're helping to keep my mind focused and stopping me from going into all-out panic. What we're doing is so incredibly dangerous, and I'm really touched these three did all this for me.

"So," I say, once there's a pause in Connor's questioning, "if this does all go to plan, and we make it across the Rip, what then?"

Connor rubs the back of his neck, clearly uncomfortable. "Well, we do have a few contingency plans. But you should know that most of them involve you and me, and likely Kriger and Merk, going into hiding. It could take us a while to build up enough evidence against Ivy. With Forra, however, we should have enough to go on, given your testimony and Ashleigh's."

"Ashleigh will testify? I know you guys said she's on our side now, but surely telling all will get her in trouble as well. Wait, is she responsible for Fram's fall?" That makes no sense to me at all and I can't believe she would go that far.

"No," says Kriger. "Ashleigh is the reason we're here; she knew about Forra's connections to Malam. Jed was the one who pushed Fram. He seems to have been Ivy's right-hand man. He's confessed to some things, but not much. I think he's hoping Ivy manages to come out of this with barely a mark against her name, and he'll be swept along for the ride." His voice turns into a growl with that remark. "Fram is keeping him with her for now. With any luck, things will start to look bad for Ivy, and Jed will use what he knows to save himself."

"What a guy," I reply. I already knew Jed was the one who knocked me out and that he's working with Forra, but I am shocked at the news that he's the one who pushed Fram. That fall was meant to kill. "Has he said why he pushed Fram?"

Connor replies, "He hasn't outright admitted to it yet, but it's pretty obvious it was him; I know he's lying every time we ask him about it. Fram and I have been doing a lot of investigative work together, and we've been suspicious of Jed for a while, as he's so close to Ivy. I'm guessing he saw Fram standing there and figured it would solve at least one of his problems." He sighs.

I try to put all these bits of information into some sort of logical order. "What about the boxes of stuff in the pillbox we found, and the guy who attacked me there? Oh, and I saw you putting very similar-looking boxes into one of the barns at the training field back in September…" I trail off at the look Connor gives me. I can't tell if he's annoyed or impressed.

"Well, to answer your first question," Connor replies, "we didn't know anything was at the pillbox until you found it. I didn't secure it in a way you might have approved of, instead I put a watch on it to see who would come and collect it. In the past, we usually just got rid of the stuff, like you apparently saw me do in Cambridge. But it wasn't getting us anywhere, so I decided that the ones you found gave us an opportunity. However, you intercepted, and knocked out, our likeliest suspect. We did question him, but we had no direct evidence he was involved, and my talent for picking out lies isn't allowed in court, so we had to let him go."

A thousand questions rush through my mind, but Kriger interjects before I can.

"Do you mean someone was watching Indigo as she was attacked and decided not to help her?" he whispers with palpable anger.

"No." Connor draws the word out slowly, trying to calm Kriger down. "That happened too far away from the pillbox, so no one saw it."

Kriger only seems partially mollified by this answer, and stands back, next to me, his arm pressing against mine. I'm surprised how comforting it feels. We haven't spoken about what we are to each other since last week, but I'm getting the impression his feelings haven't changed. Neither have mine, or at least they're back to what they were a week ago.

Minutes pass. Merk constantly checks his watch, and I'm too exhausted to ask any more questions. Silence descends upon our little group, and the bustling sound of the city feels far away. Until, that is, Connor announces it's time to leave. He walks quickly to the corner, telling us to wait for the 'all clear'

before we make our way to the doors of the imposing red brick building.

Connor gives us the signal, and I try to walk as calmly and confidently as possible, but my heart rate is making it a tad tricky. I'm hyperaware of everyone walking past us but try my best not to keep scanning for threats; it would look very suspicious. I glance up ahead at the doors in front of us and see, to my horror, Forra and five guardians walking out towards us.

Time stands still, dread pools at my feet, and I find myself bending into a fighting stance. Merk, Connor and Kriger do the same. This doesn't look good.

"Ah, Indigo, I'm so relieved to have found you, and I see you've brought some friends. Merk, Connor, always a pleasure, and this must be Kriger. Merk told me so much about you when you were born. Quite a handsome man you've become."

"You don't need to do this," says Merk.

"I don't need to do what?" replies Forra, in a mocking tone. "Stop you from taking a minor against her will through the Rip. I'm sure many people would be interested to hear how I tried my best to stop the escaped convict from killing poor, innocent Indigo, but I was just too late."

I glance around and see that most people are studiously avoiding looking at us. In fact, they're giving us a very wide berth. At least we don't need to worry about bystanders getting in the way. I have a feeling that no one here dares cross anyone for fear of being asked to live outside the city walls. The conversation has paused, and everyone seems to be waiting for someone else to make the first move. We need to keep Forra talking, to buy us some time to think up a plan.

"Do you really think you'll get away with this?" I ask. "You've created quite a web; it only takes a few strands to loosen before it all falls apart."

Forra's eyes find mine, and she shoots poison darts at me – not literally of course – making me wonder what her talents are. Really wish I'd asked Connor and Merk about that earlier.

"I am quite proud of that web actually," she replies, venom dripping from her tone. "All this work I've created is keeping a lot of people happily employed. Now I know my inheritance is secure, I can finally buy my way out of this 'web'."

I see Kriger press something on his shirt. It looks like a button, but there's something awfully familiar about it. It looks like one of the devices Ashleigh gave us when we were spying on Connor. It's got to have, at least, a microphone on it. Maybe if we can stay alive for long enough to get Forra to confess, we can use it to help lock all of those involved away.

I start peppering Forra with questions. She's getting more exasperated with me, but it's clear she's very proud of what she's achieved, and who she's managed to convince – bribe – to join her. However, it doesn't take long for her patience to wear thin. The looks of shock on Connor and Merk's faces when she tells them about my mother's death, which I was braced for, seems to please her immensely.

She waves a dismissive hand. "That's enough. I hope I've satisfied all your curiosities. Such a shame you'll have no one to share them with. Death on a distant world… It's truly tragic what accidents can occur." She smirks before gesturing for the guards around her to attack.

They come at us hard and fast. We manage to hold our own for a few minutes, but it's clear we might need some help if we're to win. If Forra joins in, then we're really screwed. As we fight, I realise Forra keeps herself well back, as if she's afraid to get involved. Merk and Connor don't even bother to attack her. Clearly, they don't think she's a physical threat. They would know. Maybe she doesn't have any special talents, which could explain why she goes to such extremes to compensate: she's jealous of those around her.

As we fight, I keep half an eye out for something I can use my Tk on. I dare not use it on a person: what if I don't lift their whole body? That could have very gross results. All I spy are lampposts, which are too far away not to be noticed if they move, and some artificial trees. In fact, there's one tree standing right behind Forra and her goons. If I can set it in motion, then I could maybe knock one or two of them unconscious, which would give us a chance.

I fight hard with one of the men, but focus on defence, so I can allow the rest of my mind to work on uprooting the tree. Although, being fake, it may not take too much effort. I try my best not to stare at it intently, and give my idea away, but to allow my mind to shift focus and lift it.

The tree, and a large chunk of pavement, rise up with remarkable ease. And noise. Everyone pauses as they turn to look and I use that moment to launch it, massively misjudging the strength required. The tree lands at Forra's feet.

She turns back to face us, I'm assuming to gloat, but in all that noise and chaos she didn't hear me approach. It's my fist she finds instead. There's a very satisfying crunch when it meets her face. Her eyes roll to the back of her head, and she drops to the ground.

The men around her look shocked to find their leader unconscious. Connor, Merk and Kriger take full advantage of their hesitancy and quickly take them out. We don't waste a moment and run for the doors of the building.

It's chaos. There are so many people here, with several of them fighting, or shouting at each other. I'm amazed to spot Fram and a few other mentors from the Academy. Connor and Merk look surprised to see them as well, so I'm guessing they weren't part of their plan. My heart swells at the thought of all these people being on our side. They appear to be winning whatever debate – fight – is going on.

Kriger and I are quickly ushered past security and to the room containing the Rip. Fram joins us and moves to the control module, which determines the Rip's destination. There's no time for any questions before I'm promptly shoved towards the doors housing the Rip. They slide open before me, and I scramble through the Rip itself. The feeling of weightlessness only lasts a few seconds, before I see the other side appear through the gloom. I walk through and am met by three armed guards.

I don't know if they're here to arrest or protect me, but the way one of them handles me and drags me away makes me think it's the former. Before I leave the room, I glance back to see Kriger walking through and receiving similar treatment. I'm escorted into the main lobby, past groups of nervous onlookers, and then outside, where I find Ivy.

She's standing there, hands on hips, with a small smirk playing on her face. She's beside some other people I vaguely recognise; my shock at seeing Ivy has addled my brain somewhat, so I don't remember who they are. They look much older than most people at the Academy, and the way they're dressed makes me think these might be the other council members. Is it time for that meeting already? Why are they here, and why on earth does Ivy look so smug? There's also a small crowd of people behind her, many of them students from the Academy. They've travelled a long way to be here. Maybe they came as backup?

Moments pass before everyone from Malam makes it through the Rip and is standing before Ivy and the others.

"I'm so pleased to see you all here together," Ivy says. "I cannot fathom why such respected members of our beloved Luenn Academy would betray us so viciously and go so far to cover it up. Not to mention luring young trainees into their schemes. Any final words from any of you before you're sent away for questioning?"

"I have a few words to say," says Kriger, stepping forward as much as his guard will allow him to.

He looks so gallant standing there; my heart aches watching him. He grabs the circular device off his shirt and throws it into the crowd. A hand reaches up to grab it, and I see Ashleigh slide the device into a tablet. Forra's voice is loud and clear, as is her image on the screen. I didn't realise Kriger's device could film as well, but I'm very relieved it did.

Everyone is silent as they take in Forra's words. Ivy looks confused and agitated as she tries to figure out what's going on. I watch her face and spot the moment she realises this is not going to end well for her. She starts shouting for someone to stop the recording, but the students standing around Ashleigh form a barrier, preventing anyone from getting near.

Once the video stops, the murmurs of the crowd are sombre indeed. Heads start turning towards Ivy, and it's clear what they all think. Quickly reading the situation, one of the members of the council, I think he represents the Americans, starts to speak. His American accent confirms my theory.

"I see we may have all been misled in this matter. Of course, we shall have a thorough investigation, but in the meantime, I think it would be prudent to release those people standing before me and take Ms Ivy Jenkins into custody." He turns to me. "My dear, I am very sorry for what has happened to you these past months, particularly this last week. I invite you and any others with information to come and speak to the members of the council, so we may get this matter fully resolved." He turns back to the crowd. "I think it best we all make a calm…"

Shouts erupt around us, and I turn to see what's happening. Forra and her men, looking a little worse for wear, have made an appearance. They're immediately caught by the guards who were holding us and brought before the council.

"Ah," says the councilman with the American accent, "how happy I am that you have come to join us. We are placing you under arrest on the grounds of treason."

"Don't be ridiculous," says Forra, her eyes blazing with fury.

The five men with her look around in panic.

"I am not the one who has committed treason. It's them you want," she cries, gesturing at me and the others.

"Of course, we shall investigate your part in this thoroughly, but recent evidence has been brought to our attention, and I shall leave it to these capable guardians to explain it all to you."

He turns his back on her and her accomplices, dismissing them entirely. Forra sputters and shouts, but she and her men are quickly escorted, along with Ivy, into another building, beside the one containing the Rip.

"As I was saying," says the councilman, "please make your way back to your homes. We shall make sure you all have transportation. Do be patient and allow the guardians to do their jobs without interference."

With that, everyone starts to disperse, although the noise of their conversation is hard to ignore. I hear people shout my name and Kriger's, but there are too many people moving around to see who it is.

I really hope that the guardians who deal with Forra and Ivy are not part of this whole mess. This thing could be a lot more complicated than any of us realise; there are certainly more people on Evig involved, which is where lots of the illegal goods are from. I take a mental step back: there's nothing I can do about that at this moment. I'll speak to the council in the coming days and then, hopefully, that'll be the end of my part in this.

A large, warm hand engulfs mine, and I look up to see Kriger's grinning face. I can't help but grin foolishly back at him. Giddy relief consumes me and I turn to leap into his arms. He chuckles and spins me around, before lowering me slowly to the ground. He gently tucks my short hair behind my ears, then bends down towards me, his face mere inches from mine, waiting silently for consent. I close my eyes and tilt my head up to receive his kiss, and revel in the feeling of his arms around me and his lips on mine. The hubbub of everyone around us disappears.

This is where I belong.

EPILOGUE

Two months later I am sitting on my garden fence, cheese toastie in hand, chatting to Cassie, who's sitting beside me. So much has happened since I joined the Luenn Academy that I hardly recognise myself. I feel far less fearful of the world around me. Perhaps a bit surprising, given what's happened, but it's because of what I went through that I feel this way. I discovered my true strength and who I could trust with my life. My hair has grown a little longer, and I've kept the red. It's a reminder of a stranger's kindness when I needed it most. And I like it.

"You in there, Indie?" Cassie teases.

"Huh? Oh yeah, sorry, I was miles away. Tell me about you. What's happened this past week?"

Cassie's expression becomes wistful and hopeful.

"There's someone new, isn't there?" I ask.

"There might be."

Cassie's ex-girlfriend, Sarah, left her shortly after I disappeared. Apparently, Cassie was so focused on figuring out what had happened to me, not believing the sudden training exercise excuse for a minute, and Sarah couldn't handle it. She had never liked me, and certainly wasn't happy about Cassie having such close ties to an OWL. It was the final straw.

"I know you already like her, so I hope you approve."

"I like her? Oh goodness, please tell me it's not Ashleigh."

Cassie has gotten to know a few of my Academy friends, as many hung out with Kriger and I every day to help us process what happened and heal together. Ashleigh and I are on speaking terms, and I do understand how she got wrapped up in all this, but I can't help feeling the remnants of betrayal. Essentially, Forra used Ivy as an intermediary to bribe Ashleigh with money. Money her family really needed. As far as Ashleigh was concerned, her role only involved keeping an eye on me – she was fed some rubbish about me being on a terrorist watch group. Her help after we got back, and during my rescue, has definitely covered most of the wound.

"Ha ha, absolutely not. No, it's Freya."

"Freya?" I'm shocked. I didn't see the two of them together much, so I'm surprised they've formed an attachment. "Cassie, that's fantastic. Freya is one of the best people I know. I'm very happy for you."

"Thank you," Cassie primly replies.

She bursts into a wild grin. Her delight is infectious, and I can't help but grin in return. I worry I've made these past few months all about me, so I'm thrilled Cassie has something wonderful happening for her.

"Ten minutes till supper!" Dad calls from behind us.

I shout back an affirmative and give Cassie a hug. My dad and I are in possibly the best place we've ever been. His hearing the full details of Elna's death, and the fact that those responsible are now behind bars, has released him from the grips of whatever prison he had put himself in. Although we cried a lot about it together, we are both so relieved to know the full story. I think he's especially relieved to know that, as long as Forra stays where she belongs, I should be safe. Well, at least from that threat.

I look up to see Kriger walking along the path towards the

house and my heart instantly picks up its pace. We've made our relationship official, which meant telling Connor. I can't say he was happy about it, but he, of course, already knew. I think he felt so bad about what we all went through that he'd forgive pretty much anything.

I shout back at Dad, "Might need to add another plate," as Kriger reaches us. He lifts me down off the fence and gives me a firm yet gentle kiss. He's now permanently living here on Earth. His parents and brother decided to explore the music scene on this world for a while, most likely to stay close to Kriger, and I couldn't be happier.

"I missed you," I say, smiling gently at him.

He smiles back. "Love you too, Indie."

Cassie coughs indiscreetly behind us.

"Although I mainly came to see you, I do have news for you both. I'm guessing you're still avoiding the news on your tablet?"

"It seems prudent to avoid a blow-by-blow account of everything," I reply. The details that keep appearing around further corruption, not to mention the daily reminders about how close I came to dying, were taking their toll.

"Well then, you haven't heard that Evig has discovered a new world."

"Really?" It has been a few years since the last discovery. "What's it like?"

"That's the thing, it also calls itself Earth. The climate there is somewhat unstable, partly due to their very large population. In fact, they have billions of people living there, nearly five times as many as here."

"Wild," I reply.

"Yeah, it's creepily similar to our Earth, even down to some of the city's names. There's another Cambridge in this same location, but Scotland is a lot smaller than ours. I mean, there are lots of differences, but the similarities are quite creepy. It's going to raise a lot of questions about parallel worlds. If we're lucky, after another year of training, we might get to visit it."

"Oh, sure," says Cassie, "because that has worked out so well for you guys in the past."

I stick my tongue out at her. Another world. My mind fills with questions. I'll be looking into it as soon as I get a chance. For now, I'm content to sit here with two of my most favourite people. Who knows what we'll face next?

"Dinner's ready!" Dad shouts.

Okay, scrap that, food first.